HOUSE OF UNSEELIE

KINGS AND QUEENS, BOOK 3

by

Kristal Dawn Harris

COPYRIGHT

Books in the Kings & Queens Series
House of Fae
House of Lycan
House of Unseelie
House of Dragon

BLURB

"She inhaled a deep breath for courage, fighting the words, but losing the battle. Love shouldn't be a war, but he stalked her on the battlefield with weapons of desire and desperation."

His senses expanded over the throng of sweaty bodies on the dance floor, searching for her. She was a beacon in the writhing madness, the soul bond enticing him toward temptation. Her lithe body swayed to the hypnotic beat, hands raised, not a care in the world. Young and beautiful, in the prime of her life, she didn't know a monster stalked her. If he had any redeeming qualities, he would leave.

Forced to return to power, The Unseelie King circled his prey. He was expected to harness this necromancer...his mate. He refuses to love again, but one glance into the haunted eyes of his fated mate, and a whirlwind of events take place he never thought imaginable. Demons want her, but will he fight to save her?

A young necromancer is the target of demonic forces. Her gifts are unique, but no match for the evil coming against her. All hope seems lost until a strange man appears on her porch surrounded by a halo of light. The ropes of his soul pierce hers and provide protection, but the tether won't hold without love. He doesn't want her, but she sees through his grumpy exterior. True emotion hides behind his black eyes, and she vows to love him hard.

As the past comes to call, love isn't easy for fated mates in House of Unseelie, the third book in the Kings & Queens series. Read it if you dare!

EXCERPT

Celine's lips twitched, and she bit the inside of her cheek. The exhaustion and nausea hadn't ceased since last Friday, after attempting communication with Mabel's dead husband. Dark-circled, red-rimmed eyes stared back from the bathroom mirror. She couldn't continue to live on crackers and soda.

Bumps in the night, doors slamming, and moans kept her awake. A few sporadic naps in the backyard gazebo were the only reason she still functioned. If she could afford to move, she would, but it wasn't possible. It required every penny she earned to pay for this house. She should sell it and relocate to a new city. Tomorrow, a call to a realtor was first on her list. With no family to help, she had no other choice.

She grabbed the tube of toothpaste off the bathroom counter and squeezed. The green, gooey substance dropped on the bathroom counter in a blob, slid off, and splattered onto the tiled floors.

Her eyes rolled to the ceiling, and she released a deep sigh just as the bathroom door slammed shut behind her. Her body jerked. Celine swiveled with annoyance, dropping her toothbrush in the sink. No one else was in the house, and the doors were locked. The windows were all closed and secured except for the one in her bathroom, but even the warm night air couldn't chase the chill in the house away.

Bare feet hesitantly slid across the tile toward the door. Her shoulders straightened. There was no way a demon was going to run her out of her home, but the hair standing at attention on the back of her neck said something else. It spoke of her fear and frustration at trying to fight something she couldn't see, an entity terrorizing her.

Thunder crashed outside just as her hand reached for the doorknob, and she quickly jerked back. Her gaze darted to the window when it vibrated and dropped with a loud bang. The glass pane shattered into jagged pieces inside her bathtub.

Exhausted, annoyed, and at the end of her rope, she was sick of whatever haunted her. Refusing to cower, Celine jerked the bathroom door open and crossed the threshold into her bedroom. Her jaw clenched in anger at finding her things on the carpet. Dresser drawers were jerked out of their places and tossed about the room. The comforter and sheets were in tatters, her clothes in messy piles, and the picture frames all shattered.

The only thing remaining upright was a lamp in the corner. Celine faced it when the lightbulb flickered. A strong breeze moved through the room, and lightning flashed outside the bedroom window. A demon's moan echoed off the walls followed by a hiss.

This was war, and the word *defeat* wasn't part of her vocabulary.

She reached for her black tourmaline necklace as a fog-like presence formed. The stone heated against her palm. Rain pelted the side of the house in a torrential downpour, the storm finally unleashing its fury.

A white flash lit the room, revealing the demon. Solid black in form, its head tilted with a sinister smirk on its mouth. Hollowed eyes glared at her, its jagged teeth snapping together. "Celine," it whispered.

The house rattled with the next clap of thunder, and she jumped. Her breath became ragged, her heart roared in her ears, and cold sweat covered her body. The blood in her veins trickled to a crawl, and her entire body shivered from terror.

Celine gripped her stone tighter, and her chin raised in defiance. This demon wouldn't possess her body, but when the lightning flashed again, it wasn't the demon with sharp teeth, but the sweet smile of her deceased mother. "Mom?" she asked, confused.

"There's a time to fight and a time to run, Celine. You've opened a portal, and I can't close it from this side. Your harnesser waits for you. Get out of the house now!"

Celine shook her head and lifted her hand just as the corporeal body of her mother vibrated, the demon's face merging with hers. It was as if they shared the same skin. Her mother's neck tilted at an abnormal angle, and visible tremors rattled her entire body. The demon screeched and fought, her mother struggling to hold it.

Blue eyes, so like her own, bore into her soul. "Run now!"

House of Unseelie
Kristal Dawn Harris

PROLOGUE

Elijah Drake hovered in the shadows beneath an overhang, glaring at the wisp of a woman called Celine. The soul bond led him to her. Now that he wore the black tourmaline, he couldn't force her from his mind. The stone warmed against his skin, expanding throughout his vampire-cold body. He should've tossed the stone in the trash, but the thought of parting with it was irksome.

She was the one all right, so why the fuck was she entering this club?

Music pulsated from the doors every time they opened. His dark gaze tracked the heels on her feet, traveled upward over shapely legs to her perfect ass, narrow waist, and the red tank barely concealing her pert breasts. A snarl rested on the corner of his lips. White hair fell softly against her back and surrounded her face. Lips painted ruby red caused his mouth to salivate with a need he didn't welcome.

He should drain her dry and leave her corpse in the alleyway behind the building. Necromancers were nothing but trouble. And this one irritated him in every way a woman could.

She had no business here. He knew the owner and spent many nights with women in concealed booths, women who thought they were something more. Salem, Massachusetts, drew the paranormal along with the fake. Maybe Celine was more like him. He almost chuckled until he saw a human male speak to her.

His body instantly tensed, and rage hummed in his veins. His incisors dropped in response to the urge to kill. Fucking hell. He'd never been jealous a day in his vampire life.

The club provided blood and sexual deviants, his personal preference, especially together. Muscles contracted, and blood rushed to his damn dick when her eyes pivoted to his location. There was no way she could see him, but she sensed him. The pull to her was stronger than anything he'd ever experienced. The confirmation, or the damning proof, arrived when she clutched the black tourmaline suspended from her neck.

Concern and confusion momentarily flashed in her expression, so he waited. Would she act on what she felt? He dared her to, seethed that fate dropped this sexy problem in his lap, allowing anger to flood her in waves. She flinched as if he'd smacked her across the face. When she turned away and entered the club, he slithered from the shadows.

The soul bond fought with his desire to leave until it won, and he casually crossed the street toward the back of the club. A door guard confronted him with an aggressive gesture, but the man was no match. Elijah attacked him before he ran, draining the lifeforce from his body. His fangs retracted from his nightly meal, and he discarded the body inside a large trash can.

The club was full of humans seeking a night of pleasure or pain. His senses expanded over the throng of sweaty bodies on the dance floor, searching for her. She was a beacon in the writhing madness, the soul bond enticing him toward temptation. Her lithe body swayed to the hypnotic beat, hands raised, not a care in the world. Young and beautiful, in the prime of her life, she didn't know a monster stalked her.

If he had any redeeming qualities, he would leave.

Their bond pulsated in waves, tugging at his soul. He could drain her perfect body of its essence and rid himself of the impulse by midnight, but the idea festered on his tongue.

She turned her back to him, and his eyes lowered to her curvy ass, swaying to the beat. The music changed to a sultry pop song with hauntingly seductive notes. Small hands lifted thick hair from her neck, and he flicked his tongue against a pointed incisor. Another male approached and circled her, propelling him onto the dance floor.

The sea of bodies parted, creating a path for him as he shadowed his prey, sliding behind and close enough to touch her. He could span the width of her waist with his hands, started to, but her arms lifted over her head.

The crowd sighed when black magic particles expanded from her fingertips, caressing everyone including him. His eyes closed with a hiss of contempt. This necromancer defined sin with her sultry movements, parted lips, and hooded eyes. Couples moved closer, kissed with frenzy, and rubbed together, heightening the sensual vibe in the club.

Spirits bombarded the building to hover on the ceiling, seeking her, lured by her necromancer magic. Corporeal bodies slid over the crowd, circling from above once they located her. His jaw clenched. Fucking ghosts. They didn't differ from him in their need to be close to her, and it pissed him off more. If the patrons weren't under her spell, they'd scream in fright. She didn't know the havoc she wrought with her gift.

His little necromancer was the perfect storm.

He growled at the seduction tugging him closer, his black soul responding to the spell she weaved. It encircled him in a sticky web he couldn't escape. A sliver of his old magic rose from his body, shocking him. The necromancer coaxed it from his soul, even though he hadn't experienced it since the day a curse changed him forever.

His magic bound to hers above the people. Couples disappeared for secluded corners as the magic intensified their most wicked desires.

She pivoted to him with her eyes glazed black as the midnight sky. The necromancer's need for the harnesser recognized him even if the woman didn't, but he no longer possessed the gift. One dainty hand lifted to touch his chest, and she moved closer, her hips rolling in invitation.

Unable to resist, he jerked her into his body and leaned over her smaller frame. She should run from him, scream, or push him away, but she molded to his body like she was always meant to be there. His mouth rested against her neck, nose trailing along her flesh, inhaling her sweet floral scent deeply. Incisors lengthened, scraping gently against her throat. A bead of blood soaked into his tongue, but the man ached for more. She sighed in his arms, an addictive sound of surrender.

Her hands linked behind his neck, and they were one.

Heaven and hell on the dance floor.

He traced the shape of her body, licking his lips at the tempting flesh. Her pelvis rocked against his dick until he was hard as a stone. Small breasts pressed into his chest. Desire elevated to reckless lust, and people kissed and moaned in wild abandon. Her neck tilted in an unaware, innocent offering. His eyes narrowed on her quivering pulse point, throbbing for him to finish her.

The soul bond dared him and laughed in his face. It would be so easy to end this torment, but he couldn't do it.

When the song faded, her face lifted. The ghosts above them departed through the ceiling. Black eyes, necromancer eyes, dropped to his chest where the tourmaline hung. She licked her lips nervously and reached to touch it, but he backed away before she made contact.

"No," he sneered, tilting his head at his adversary. Fuck no. The bond screamed to grab her, lift her straddled on his waist, and claim her right here, right now, but he forced it under control. He didn't want this.

Destiny just claimed an advantage in the war, tricking him like the bitch she was.

Chapter 1

The fragrance of roses saturated the small dining room. It was a sign of the dead's presence and could be pleasant or odorous, depending on the soul. The chandelier swayed as a strong breeze blew through the space, circled both occupants, and peacefully settled. Dim lights flickered and cast shadows to slide across the walls.

The whisper of something that shouldn't be in the living realm caressed Celine's cheek. Her palms twitched on the dining room table, and, with the slight tilt of her head, she waited for an invitation.

It wasn't polite to barge your way into the world of the dead. She kept her aura peaceful, tempting the soul with her gift. It wanted to communicate, or it wouldn't be here. The spirit brushed against her arm, cool and gentle. A whispering moan echoed in the room. It was time.

Her eyes closed at the same moment a deep breath left her parted lips. Her soul transitioned to hover just behind the chair her physical body occupied. The eyes of her separated spirit opened immediately, and she searched for the entity, the departed man she sought.

Celine located his smoky-gray form in a dark corner of the dining room. He nodded once and slowly ascended through the ceiling until his essence was undetectable. She allowed her soul to follow the soul of the man into the place where all spirits dwelled, into the Domain of Souls.

Her astral projection halted in the lower domain. To go any further could spell disaster for one such as herself, a living medium. It wasn't her time to pass, so her soul still belonged in her physical body.

Because she could easily lose her way or the desire to return, her time was limited in this place. The lower domain served as a welcoming platform with a serene-like atmosphere. It calmed the spirits, allowing them to accept their new state of being before ascending into the middle domain.

Celine's gaze lifted. Millions of souls wandered in the milky-white space above her head, the middle domain. They shuffled back and forth, with no purpose in their silent steps. These spirits hadn't yet elevated into the place of peace, or the upper domain, and lingered for many reasons.

Some died unexpectedly, not realizing they were dead, some had unfinished business with living loved ones, and some died too early by nefarious means. Some entities were filled with rage and some with restlessness.

There were many reasons the soul of a person didn't elevate into the upper domain. She understood and accepted their reasons without judgment, straining to hear the jumbled words they murmured.

Attuned to the spirit that entered her home, Celine politely waited for the message her client sought. She studied his form among the sea of spirits, not understanding why he invited her, but now seemed evasive. The grayish entity slid back and forth among the other spirits, remaining within her sight. Her corporeal form floated forward until he slowly ascended into the middle domain.

Unease crept along her spine when the soft-spoken words suddenly turned into moans and shrieks from hundreds of spirit voices. Never had she been afraid in this realm, but fear laced with panic overwhelmed her spirit. Her gaze didn't stray from the soul-frothed sea above her face as she slowly backed away.

A wispy hand unexpectedly dropped from the mass of souls, and Celine paused. Her head tilted, studying the hand. She floated in the abyss, trying to determine which spirit it belonged to. Her weightless hand lifted, but she hesitated.

Her instincts screamed this wasn't right, and she'd been warned by her mother about the middle domain, but this was the reason she came. There was no room for doubt. Her client paid her money for this gift, and she couldn't return to her body without an answer.

Who murdered this man and why?

Celine grasped the hand and immediately regretted her decision. Cold slithered over her corporeal skin, attempting to engulf her soul. The hand tugged as the spiritual moans intensified. The grip of the hand strengthened.

She attempted to jerk away without success. Her soul lifted toward the middle domain against her will. The polite invitation morphed into a spiritual attack in three seconds. She should've listened to her instincts. The spirit of the man wasn't what he seemed. This wasn't the peaceful presence in her home.

More hands dropped as she neared the barrier separating the lower and middle domains. Terror seeped deeper into her soul when her head breached the divide. Unfriendly fingers slithered across and through her spiritual skin, squeezing as they latched onto her arms and shoulders. These entities shouldn't be here. They hadn't accepted their deaths or made any kind of peace, clinging to rage. Never had she experienced such evil in the spiritual realm.

Afraid of what she would witness, Celine closed her eyes. She didn't want to see what waited for her. Once her entire soul entered the middle domain, the moans and screams immediately stopped, and the hands latched onto her soul faded into nothing. Eerie silence filled the void where a few moments ago the voices were undiscernible.

She fumbled to grasp the black tourmaline suspended from her neck on a silver chain, whispering a silent prayer for strength, guidance, and protection to whatever deity might be listening. Her eyelids slowly lifted, expecting the worst, but there wasn't anything except the whitish expanse of the middle domain. No souls remained besides hers, floating weightlessly in the abyss.

Minutes passed before the screams began again. Celine cringed, waiting for the evil to reveal itself when a black form appeared in her field of vision. She strained to make out the entity rushing toward her.

Bracing herself as best she could, Celine held her breath until a mouthful of sharp teeth snapped right before her face. She gasped and tried to slide backward, but the demonic soul wrapped its thin arms around her body and refused to let go. A scream erupted, riding over the souls.

The demon hissed close to her ear, whispering vile words until she thought her head would explode. Its razor-sharp teeth clicked together, followed by a menacing laugh. "You'll be the vessel by which I enter the realm of the living, Celine."

She wrestled against the demonic force holding her as anger, retaliation, and repulsion churned in her spirit. "You can't possess a soul, demon!"

The demon chuckled, strengthening its hold on her soul. "Stupid necromancer. You have no harnesser, so I've tethered to you."

Blackness saturated the realm in an instant. Celine closed her eyes tightly and prayed with renewed vigor. The potent scent of sulfur surrounded her and seeped into her nostrils with each labored breath. The back of her throat and her eyes burned. Coughs wracked her along with the demon's tight hold, surely bruising her soul. Dizziness swiftly assaulted her mind even though she couldn't see, and her stomach rolled with nausea.

This was it. She would die in this place, possibly consumed with disgust and unable to find peace like the one latched onto her corporeal body. She sucked in one last breath and gagged before all conscious thought fled her mind, succumbing to sheer terror.

On a scream, she lifted her head from the dining room table, coming face to face with her client's terrified expression. Confusion replaced her fear. She didn't remember leaving the Domain of Souls, but here she sat with her client in her dining room.

She wanted to ease the fear on the woman's face, but her stomach cramped, forcing her to lurch over the side of the table. Bile burned in her throat, and nausea caused her mouth to fill with water. The contents of her stomach met the floor.

A neatly folded paper towel appeared in her vision just as she finished. Mortified, Celine plopped back into her chair with a sigh of exhaustion. "Thank you. I'm so sorry, Mabel. I don't know what happened. One minute I followed your husband's soul into the lower domain, and the next, a demon attacked. I was lucky to re-enter my body."

Mabel wrung her hands repeatedly. "Did he tell you anything?"

"No, nothing. I didn't even speak with him. It was the oddest thing. I'm not even sure that was him."

Still nauseous and slightly disoriented, Celine laid her head against the high-back chair to study Mabel. Suspicious eyes narrowed on her client, her disheveled appearance, and the way she avoided eye contact. Mabel seemed anxious, with underlying guilt behind her eyes. Her shoulders hunched, and she glanced away. This woman withheld information. "Are you sure there's nothing you can tell me about your husband's murder? We've been doing this for months without answers."

"No, nothing else."

Celine frowned when Mabel laid a hundred-dollar bill on the table and quickly rose from her seat. In an obvious hurry to leave, she stumbled on the leg of the table but glanced over her shoulder. "Next Friday at the same time?"

"I'll pencil you in my appointment book."

With Mabel's departure, Celine sighed deeply and closed her eyes. The hour was late, but it was the confrontation with the demon that drained her energy. The life of a psychic medium wasn't an easy one.

Necromancer was her former title, but people didn't response well to the word.

In the last year, six demonic entities confronted her while traveling in the Domain of Souls, but none as strong as this one. Those demons were ruining her business and forcing her to reconsider offering her services.

Her fingers absently caressed the black tourmaline pendant suspended from her neck. The stone always protected her from evil but seemed to weaken each moment she spent in the Domain of Souls, or the demon's gained strength. Either way, she would have to be more careful when traveling in her astral body.

Her mother warned her about these things during her training, but this confrontation seemed personal. The terms "tethered" and "harnessed" were new.

Celine's gaze darted to the dust-covered Book of Necromancy lying on its side in the bookcase. She didn't bother to continue her studies after her mother passed away, but maybe it was time. She'd have to do it herself, which was dangerous, but there wasn't another choice. No coven would help her.

Considered an outcast, she didn't fit in anywhere. Labeled a necromancer, no one would work with her. The local coven called her gift black magic, and the birthmark on her inner wrist their confirmation. The dark slash meant nothing to her, but apparently it was a sign. Her mother bore the same mark.

With hands firmly planted on the table, Celine rose from her chair on shaky legs. She stumbled into the kitchen for wipes to clean her mess off the floor. With a sigh of exhaustion, she dropped to her knees.

After finishing, she used the chair to pull herself upright. A door slammed upstairs, and she froze. Her eyes lifted to the second floor, and her head tilted, listening. When nothing else happened, she chuckled to herself. Her tired mind played tricks on her. A good night's rest would rejuvenate her body, and tomorrow she'd study her mother's ancient book.

Chapter 2

Cool dirt cocooned his body when the Druid Council's magic tingled on his skin. It was a summons Elijah ignored repeatedly over the last two days. He hadn't approached Celine since the night at the club, and refused to answer the call when he experienced her magnifying fear. The tourmaline heated, close to burning his chest. He'd rather be branded before bowing to the fucking soul bond.

Bitterness and rage consumed him, and the Druid Council bore the blame. Who were they to call him back now? Fuck them, and their righteous attitudes. The image of the woman's haunting features taunted his mind and tugged at his soul, the bond between them refusing to be ignored, strengthening day by day.

A snarl lifted the corner of his lips. At one time, he was the harnesser she needed, but events changed him, and the consequences couldn't be reversed.

The Druid magic faded. He settled deeper into the ground where nothing could reach him, gloating at his victory. Dirt funneled above his face and flew into the air. A hole appeared over his place of rest. A surge of energy ripped him from the earth with enough force to level a building. He thudded to the ground, his face lifting to the headstones in the graveyard. Magic pulsated, swirling his body. A harnesser's rope surrounded his waist, jerking him to his feet. Levitating in midair, a portal opened, and the unseen hand yanked him inside.

He landed in the foyer of the Druid Council, clean and fully clothed. His gaze lifted to the double doors. Disgust seeped from every cell in his body.

"I fucking hate this place," he grumbled, pushing off his knees and strolling inside the open chamber. The confrontation couldn't be avoided. That wasn't an invitation. That was a demand.

Muscles flexed and his shoulders rolled before he settled in the single seat provided, facing the Druid Council. Summoned, no kidnapped by the council, had aggravation frothing from his black soul. His head lifted to meet the glares of ten robed members perched on their lofty podium.

The unified effect would intimidate the most advanced of harnessers, but Elijah huffed in annoyance. It wasn't customary to speak without being addressed first, and he didn't have anything to say, so he waited. Long fingers tapped a rhythmic beat on the arm of the chair. He refused to lower his gaze, staring at each one in utter contempt. If he knew he'd survive, he'd drain them to shriveling corpses on the floor, and piss on their withered bodies.

Minutes passed, but no one spoke. Elijah shifted in his uncomfortable chair. Druid symbols lined the walls, the ceiling, and the floor, and energy hummed in the room. It had been a long time since he viewed this hallowed space, and he didn't belong here.

This chamber was impenetrable, and the council members were the most powerful Druids left on the planet. What could they possibly want from him? But he knew the answer to that question from Bianca...fucking goddess.

His gaze darted to the tall wooden doors when they parted slightly to allow the slight frame of an elderly necromancer entrance. Stooped over a walking stick, she shuffled across the floor to accept a seat at the edge of the council's podium.

He adjusted slightly when one of the council members cleared his throat. "Your harnesser talents are required, Elijah."

"No. You know what happened last time. My necromancer died."

"She wasn't meant for you, and she wasn't a necromancer."

Elijah jerked to the old woman's gravelly voice. "She was everything to me, and I failed her. You know nothing, old crone!"

Multiple grumblings began on the podium, but she stomped her walking stick against the floor several times, gaining everyone's attention. "I spoke to Laura myself in the spiritual realm."

Elijah jumped from his chair. "Impossible. You have no harnesser. He died years ago."

Strong wind ripped through the room, and papers flew off the podium, landing haphazardly on the floor. His hair smacked against his cheeks and neck, but he refused to apologize or cower before this necromancer. She may be his elder, she may have unbelievable power in that aged body, but Laura loved him as much as he loved her. "Laura wouldn't betray me."

He barely spoke the words, but the necromancer must've heard them because she faced him with fire in her still-intelligent eyes. She shuffled to stand before him, a scowl marring her wrinkled face.

"Laura wasn't yours to claim, nor were you hers. You went against the council and because of that rebellion, she is dead, and you live with a curse. You should've waited for your true partner in this life. Do not test me, harnesser!"

Elijah jerked as if smacked because it was true. He and Laura had been young, full of pride and passion, and he refused to listen to the council's advice. She may not have been his soul bond, but he loved her in every way a man could love a woman. His dark gaze burned as he met the old woman's glare. "I loved her."

The necromancer's face tilted, the wind continuing to whip her stringy hair in her face. "It was an immature love and a false love. She used you, harnesser. The one meant to be your soulmate in this life needs you. Will you deny her your heart? Will you deny her your protection, Unseelie King?"

His head shook, and his eyes narrowed to thin slits. "I'll never love again, and I'm no king."

She clucked her tongue, and the wind in the room settled. "Just because you say it doesn't make it so. You're the true King of the Unseelie. If you can't love her, then harness her soul before irreparable damage is done. Already, she's a target for demonic forces. They singled her out because of her unique gifts. She's been entering the Domain of Souls without a harnesser, without you to tether her."

Elijah swore and dropped into his seat. His head fell back with a groan until all he could see was the stone ceiling covered in protective symbols. Wood splintered on the arms of the chair where his hands gripped it tightly. There was no doubt this necromancer was in trouble. Her gift revealed itself to him, branded him, lured him, and he experienced her terror and passion.

Rumors and whispers about increased demonic activity in the realm of living had grown stronger over the last year. Even in the Fae realm, the rumors reached his ears, and he confirmed it from the witch's blood when he killed her. A deep sigh fell from his lips as he faced the old necromancer again. "I haven't harnessed in years, not since you punished me to exist as a fucking vampire."

Her wrinkled hand waved in the air. "You'll remember what to do when the time comes. A handsome Unseelie King like yourself shouldn't be wasting your talents feeding on blood and stupid dark witches, motivated by greed for a power they'll never comprehend."

Elijah's lips twitched. The old crone called him handsome, and he almost liked it. She also issued a challenge in the same breath.

"Celine James lives in Salem, Massachusetts."

Chuckling to himself, Elijah rose from his chair, intending to leave. He knew where Celine lived and couldn't break away from her since he saw her face and touched the damn stone.

The old woman pointed her finger at his chest where the black tourmaline lay hidden from everyone's view. "You wear her talisman. You've already connected with her. Shame on you, harnesser."

Elijah hesitated before sliding his hand over the tourmaline resting against his chest. He wanted to deny it, but there wasn't any point. His gaze rose from the floor to the old woman's smirk. She knew and gloated over her victory. "You manipulative bitch. You cursed me and now you want my help. Why not just curse her like you did me and save everyone the effort?"

The crone grinned, exposing her toothless gums. "The council has agreed to lift the curse. You won't feed on blood anymore. It's time for the Unseelie King to return."

"Well, this Unseelie is out of here."

"I don't think so," the crone snarled.

Intense heat fired in his body, and he fell to his knees on the floor at the crone's feet. Cramps sliced through his abdomen, and he groaned. Muscles tensed, and his gut burned like the flames of hell existed inside him. The stench of old blood filled his nostrils. His throat stung, and he gagged when bile coated his tongue, heaving where he kneeled. His mouth opened, expelling his last meal on the floor. Blood soaked the symbol covered tiles, shivers wracked his body, and sweat coated his skin. A wave of dizziness sent him tumbling onto his side with a pitiful moan. "You could've warned me."

The crone cackled, staring down her nose at him. "Where's the fun in that?"

He jerked when Druid symbols burned and branded his skin from the top of his head to the soles of his feet. The scent of singed flesh filled his nostrils, and his stomach lurched again. Spent and exhausted, he rolled onto his back and lifted his hand in front of his face. He proudly wore the symbols once, but they were now a reminder of all he'd lost.

"You fucking wrinkly bitch," he snarled.

"Quit your whining, Elijah Drake. We did you a favor."

"I hate all of you."

"I hope your punishment taught you a lesson, harnesser."

"It taught me that whoring and bloodlust are fantastic, and you suck gigantic balls. It was better to be a vampire."

The crone whacked him in the stomach with her stick. "You had your fill of revenge and bitterness, harnesser."

He glared at the old woman making his life a living hell. "All this time, and I don't know your name, even though you've cursed me twice."

"Nor do you need to know. My work is done. You have your assignment. Get on your feet and use your gift. And if you ignore your necromancer, I'll deliver you myself."

Elijah sneered, watching her shuffle from the chamber while using the chair to rise to his feet. Once she departed, he turned on his boot heel, slipping in the blood, before regaining his balance. He limped his broke ass from the chamber, grumbling to himself. "Fuck you all," he yelled, lifting both arms over his head with his bloody middle fingers raised.

The double doors closed with a resounding bang behind him. With one hand, he rubbed his sore stomach and inhaled a cleansing breath. The door to the outside opened, and he started to duck and hide when he realized he wasn't a vampire anymore.

With one hand shielding his eyes, he stared into the sunlight breaching the horizon. A smile spread when the warm rays caressed his face. It was the first time he'd looked upon the sun in years.

The tourmaline warmed against his chest. He winced and rolled his eyes to the ceiling when another symbol burned and formed on his inner forearm. "Fucking necromancer," he hissed, his arm stinging.

He would protect and harness her, but he vowed not to love her.

Chapter 3

Celine's lips twitched, and she bit the inside of her cheek. The exhaustion and nausea hadn't ceased since last Friday, after attempting communication with Mabel's dead husband. Dark-circled, red-rimmed eyes stared back from the bathroom mirror. She couldn't continue to live on crackers and soda.

Bumps in the night, doors slamming, and moans kept her awake. A few sporadic naps in the backyard gazebo were the only reason she still functioned. If she could afford to move, she would, but it wasn't possible. It required every penny she earned to pay for this house. She should sell it and relocate to a new city. Tomorrow, a call to a realtor was first on her list. With no family to help, she had no other choice.

She grabbed the tube of toothpaste off the bathroom counter and squeezed. The green, gooey substance dropped on the bathroom counter in a blob, slid off, and splattered onto the tiled floors.

Her eyes rolled to the ceiling, and she released a deep sigh just as the bathroom door slammed shut behind her. Her body jerked. Celine swiveled with annoyance, dropping her toothbrush in the sink. No one else was in the house, and the doors were locked. The windows were all closed and secured except for the one in her bathroom, but even the warm night air couldn't chase the chill in the house away.

Bare feet hesitantly slid across the tile toward the door. Her shoulders straightened. There was no way a demon was going to run her out of her home, but the hair standing at attention on the back of her neck said something else. It spoke of her fear and frustration at trying to fight something she couldn't see, an entity terrorizing her.

Thunder crashed outside just as her hand reached for the doorknob, and she quickly jerked back. Her gaze darted to the window when it vibrated and dropped with a loud bang. The glass pane shattered into jagged pieces inside her bathtub.

Exhausted, annoyed, and at the end of her rope, she was sick of whatever haunted her. Refusing to cower, Celine jerked the bathroom door open and crossed the threshold into her bedroom. Her jaw clenched in anger at finding her things on the carpet. Dresser drawers were jerked out of their places and tossed about the room. The comforter and sheets were in tatters, her clothes in messy piles, and the picture frames all shattered.

The only thing still upright was a lamp in the corner. Celine faced it when the lightbulb flickered. A strong breeze moved through the room, and lightning flashed outside the bedroom window. A demon's moan echoed off the walls followed by a hiss.

This was war, and the word *defeat* wasn't part of her vocabulary.

She reached for her black tourmaline necklace as a fog-like presence formed. The stone heated against her palm. Rain pelted the side of the house in a torrential downpour, the storm finally unleashing its fury.

A white flash lit the room, revealing the demon. Solid black in form, its head tilted with a sinister smirk on its mouth. Hollowed eyes glared at her, its jagged teeth snapping together. "Celine," it seethed in a gravelly voice.

The house rattled with the next clap of thunder, and she jumped. Her breath became ragged, her heart roared in her ears, and cold sweat covered her body. The blood in her veins trickled to a crawl, and her entire body shivered with terror.

Celine gripped her stone tighter, and her chin raised in defiance. This demon wouldn't possess her body, but when the lightning flashed again, it wasn't the demon with sharp teeth, but the sweet smile of her deceased mother. "Mom?" she asked, confused.

"There's a time to fight and a time to run, Celine. You've opened a portal, and I can't close it from this side. Your harnesser waits for you. Get out of the house now!"

Celine shook her head and lifted her hand just as the corporeal body of her mother vibrated, the demon's face merging with hers. It was as if they shared the same skin. Her mother's neck tilted at an abnormal angle, and visible tremors rattled her. The demon screeched and fought, her mother struggling to hold it.

Blue eyes, so like her own, bore into her soul. "Run now!"

She hit the bedroom door in a dead sprint. Pictures and candle sconces fell off the walls. The house shook from top to bottom when she rounded the balustrade on the stairs. Doors repeatedly opened and closed throughout the house. Plates and cups in the kitchen broke into a million pieces on the original hardwood floors, but still she ran.

Hot, fetid breath stung her shoulder and filled her nostrils. The sting of her hair almost ripped from her scalp brought a strangled cry. Celine tore the front door open. Icy fingers dug into the tender flesh on her upper arms when she emerged onto the front porch.

Bright white light blinded her, thunder clapped, and she froze in place. She thought it was lightning until the demon screeched in her ear and ducked behind her. Nails scratched her lower back, scraping and burning her flesh, but the demon refused to release its hold.

An enormous man dominated the steps of her porch, feet braced shoulder width apart. Wavy, white hair lifted and floated. Obsidian black eyes, darker than the stormy night raging outside her home, locked with hers.

Spellbound in the moment, Celine couldn't move. The demon's breath heated the skin on her back. A spindly arm wrapped around her waist and tightened until she could barely inhale.

"It's you," she whispered in a choked voice.

The man raised his hands in front of him. White light leaped from his palms, ropes extending from his fingers to circle her body. A halo of radiant energy outlined his form, and the demon growled against her spine.

Celine's gaze slid over his tall frame, not believing her eyes. He stepped fully onto her porch and approached until he towered above her. Her chin lifted. Dark eyes met her fear, chasing the simmering terror away with his presence. White light sparked from his black eyes, penetrated her soul, and tingled underneath her skin. She jerked from the connection, and peace replaced fear as evil cowered in the shadows.

The stranger's gaze didn't leave hers, but he spoke to the demon in an authoritative tone. "I harnessed her to me. You can't have her, demon."

The demon moaned, but its hold slackened from her waist. Time halted. Thunder rumbled low and deep. Water gushed from the gutters onto the lawn. The rain slowed to a steady pace off the porch.

His essence brushed her spirit, asking for permission, and she surrendered to his shielding touch without protest. The demon's clutch released immediately, and Celine slumped against the man's chest. His light completely enveloped her in warmth and protection. The torment was finally over.

Unable to muster the strength to lift her head or stand on her own two feet, she burrowed against the man's chest. His clean, masculine scent soothed her battered soul. Strong arms scooped beneath her legs, cradling her body into his. His gaze lowered to hers before striding inside her home.

The front door closed on the dissipating storm, ending the most horrible night of her life.

*****

Elijah studied the colonial style home, from the inviting front porch to the second floor. The tourmaline burned against his chest. Tree limbs scratched and swayed in the approaching storm, wind whipping through the property. The house sat on a cliff, and the ocean churned below, waves crashing against the rocky shore with enough force he tasted salt on his lips.

Lightning flashed in the night sky. Black tar descended over the front of the house, marring the pristine ocean blue color. A lamp flickered in one of the second-floor rooms. Glass shattered, reaching his ears even over the storm. A demon's shrill scream pierced the night.

Elijah shrugged his broad shoulders. "For fuck's sake," he grumbled. "What a damn mess."

It had been years since he'd harnessed anyone, and the necromancer was up to her neck in demonic trouble. Just as one foot contacted the first of three steps, the front door ripped open so hard it almost broke the hinges.

His breath caught in his lungs and slowly released. Lightning streaked, illuminating her frightened eyes and the unique shade of blue instead of the black he'd seen in the club. Her head jerked when the demon chasing her grasped her hair, and an arm snaked her waist.

Anger boiled over, and the gift of the harnesser soared to life.

Summoning his soul and focusing his strength, his life force extended to touch hers. She couldn't move, locked in the demon's grip, so he climbed the remaining steps until he poised before her.

Her gaze rose to his, pleading for help. Dark blemishes circled her eyes, and exhaustion marred her pale features that weren't there before. A twinge of guilt infiltrated his mind, but he pushed it aside. Protectiveness rose swift and deadly, without mercy for anything or anyone. He didn't acknowledge the demon's presence, focusing entirely on *his* necromancer.

"Do you accept me, Celine?"

The demon screamed in outrage, but Elijah didn't care. Fucking demons. Instead, he waited for her permission. "Help," she croaked in a hoarse voice.

Energy swelled, and the soul bond strengthened by the millisecond. The ropes of his soul secured about her waist and tightened. Demonic moans intensified from every direction, but he ignored them and quickly harnessed what belonged to him.

The demon disappeared in an instant, and the sweet smell of vanilla and lilacs filled his nostrils. Elijah inhaled deeply before scooping his necromancer into his arms. He paused in the doorway, studying the damage from the landing on the second floor to the ground level.

A contented sigh brought his attention back to the small woman in his arms. His little necromancer waged war. A smirk lifted the corner of his lip, and his dead heart stuttered when she hesitantly smiled back and whispered, "Thank you."

Elijah hefted his small package in his arms, searching for a soft spot to lay her. A ratty couch sat before a stone hearth. It would have to do. Just as he placed her on the sofa, a door upstairs slammed shut. Celine scrambled off the couch and latched onto his neck. "Don't leave me alone in this house."

He ran a calming hand down the back of her head, attempting to ease the fear. She huddled into his chest when another door banged on the ground floor level. Whispers surrounded them, demonic chanting. Candlesticks, books, and a vase of flowers hit the floor with a thud. Windows rattled throughout the house, allowing remnants from the storm inside. Rain sprinkled the floors. The curtains billowed horizontally.

"How many, Celine?"

She shook her head against his chest. She couldn't or wouldn't raise her head. "I don't know how many. They followed me here from the Domain of Souls."

Elijah grasped her by the waist and gathered her flush against him, tightening his arms around her back. "Listen to me. Your soul is now tethered to mine. No spirit or demon can possess you unless you invite it. I need the warrior to come back. These things will harass you until they control your life by fear."

"Who are you?"

"You're harnesser. My name is Elijah Drake."

Celine nodded against his chest. "I don't know what a harnesser is, but please don't leave me here." Several seconds passed before she lifted a tear-stained face. Exhausted and scared out of her mind, she couldn't take much more.

Elijah gazed into her angelic face, momentarily caught in the sadness of her watery eyes. She didn't know, and he didn't have time to explain when another door slammed upstairs. "Where is your Druid coven? Why aren't they helping you?"

Pink lips twitched, and she shrugged, glancing around the room with wide eyes. "I belong to no coven. My mother died when I was eighteen. She left me this house and her Book of Necromancy, but never finished training me. I tried a witch coven, but they think I'm cursed because of this mark."

Elijah scowled when she held her arm up, showing him the Druid symbol for necromancy. It matched the one recently branded on his arm, but she didn't need to know yet. A partly trained necromancer somehow brought quite a few demons back from the Domain of Souls.

His gaze lowered to her frightened face. This woman needed his protection, and he would give it without losing his heart. "The only thing I know to do is return them where they came from, but you're in no shape to do it. The mark isn't a curse, it's a gift."

Celine shook her head. "I won't go back. These things were waiting for me the last time."

"Why would they be waiting for a partly trained necromancer?" he asked.

"I don't know."

Elijah tried to stand. He needed to pace while he thought, but Celine refused to let go of his jacket. "We must leave this house until we know why these things want you, and until you're strong enough to send them back. Is there anything you want to take?"

Her frightened eyes flicked to the stairway before darting to the bookshelf. "My mother's book."

"I don't know which book belonged to your mother, so you're going to have to let go. I'll be right back."

His gaze turned to the front door when it rattled and creaked open. Celine's grip on his jacket tightened.

The door paused, caught in an invisible grip, and banged shut, the knob still turning back and forth. Everything left on the walls crashed to the floor. Elijah frowned at the attempt to frighten him, but it worked on Celine. She was too young for this type of bullshit. What the fuck was going on here?

He had no other option but to lift Celine from the couch and shelter her against his body. "Show me which book."

The bookshelf shifted at their approach, scraping the floor. One eyebrow arched. These demons didn't want Celine to have her mother's book. Why? An unanswered question he would understand, eventually. Right now, he needed to get Celine out of this house before her heart burst from her chest.

Flames leaped in the hearth, a fire roaring without wood, and pushed outward. Books fell to the floor as they neared until he stood before the antique cabinet. Celine held onto him for dear life. "You have to show me," he whispered into her ear.

She barely tilted her face, just enough to point out the book. Once he grabbed it and stuffed it between his chest and her body, he pivoted to the front door. The entire house groaned. Moans and screeches erupted from everywhere. Doors on both floors opened and slammed repeatedly.

Elijah didn't glance at anything other than the exit from this hellhole, and he didn't let go of Celine. As his hand reached for the doorknob, the heated glare from multiple demons pierced his back. Legion. More than one demon haunted this house and wanted his necromancer. The fine hairs on his neck rose to attention, but he refused to show fear.

It angered them he was here and removing Celine. A scratch burned his back and another on his neck. Cold hands attempted to reach for his soul. A smirk lifted his lips. They couldn't do anything to him, and they certainly couldn't latch to his soul. A scratch was nothing and would instantly heal. Elijah grinned. He shrugged his shoulders and tightened one arm possessively around Celine's shivering body. With his free hand, he jerked the door open a little too hard. Chin held high, he paused before crossing over the threshold. "Do your worst. There's no fear left in me, demons, for I haven't anything else to lose."

With that statement, he crossed the doorway onto the front porch. The door banged shut behind him. He marched down the steps, the eerie sound of things crashing to the floor in the unoccupied house.

Elijah's lips lifted in a half smile, but he didn't look behind him. They wanted the acknowledgement he wouldn't give. Let them throw their tantrum, without terrorizing Celine.

*****

After he deposited her on the sidewalk like a sack of potatoes, Celine stared at the beast of a man who rescued her. She remembered him from the dance club, but never thought of seeing him again after the way he acted.

White hair fell to his waist, but his eyes were as black as the night sky. A black button-up shirt and leather jacket accentuated his wide shoulders and chest, but his muscular body tapered at the waist. Dark jeans outlined long, thick legs, and he wore black boots. He stood at least a foot over her with scarred symbols on every inch of exposed skin. Her eyes widened at his pointed ears. "You're Fae?"

"What do you know of the Fae?" he barked, facing her.

"Not much except they exist." She jerked to the house when it shook from the roof to the foundation. Elijah moved behind her. She backed into his chest. A scream split the night, windows exploded outward, fire engulfed the structure, and multiple demons burst from every direction.

"Holy shit. Time to go," Elijah yelled, tucking the book inside his shirt.

"Go where?"

"Druid Council."

She didn't argue when he swiveled her and lifted her by the waist, yanked her into his chest, and a circle of light opened beside him. The light seemed to move in and out on both sides before stabilizing. Celine ducked her head to his chest when he stepped inside.

"Hold on, Celine."

She didn't need to be told twice and held on for dear life as they traveled somewhere, but anywhere was better than her home. Those things were determined to capture her.

They landed on a grassy lawn outside a dilapidated building, but the circle of people caught her attention. White hooded robes covered each one. She couldn't see their faces, but they were in pairs.

Elijah set her down. The ground vibrated. Her gaze lifted. "Are we safe?"

"Not yet."

She heard the screech behind them. He grabbed her hand and began running, pulling her along at the same time.

"Inside the circle," he yelled.

She glanced over her shoulder, and her eyes widened in fear. Demons charged across the lawn. Their corporeal forms were grayish-black as they desperately reached for her, arms extended, and spindly fingers ready to grab.

The moment she crossed into the circle, power like she'd never experienced covered her. The people in robes clapped one time in unison, lifted their hands, and a white shield rose from the earth to create a dome.

Celine gasped when the demons slammed into it repeatedly without breaching it. They whispered her name, circling the dome, their forms brushing against the barrier and testing it, searching for a way inside.

"Celine, come to us. Must have the queen," they chanted in unison.

She covered her ears when the chanting became wails and screams. "Make them stop," she pleaded.

*****

For the first time, Elijah was at a loss. In all his experience, walking in the human realm and the Fae realm, he'd seen nothing like it. This was a legion of demons, a small army that refused to quit. The moment he harnessed her, they should've left.

They knew her name, which wasn't uncommon, but they also knew she was a queen...his queen. The knowledge made him question everything he thought he knew.

One hand slid over her head and down her back as she pressed against him with her hands over her ears. This was torture for her, and he couldn't stop it.

The harnesser power rose in protectiveness when he didn't want it to. White strands of light expanded from his soul to surround them both. They couldn't penetrate the Druid shield, but he still had the urge to shelter her.

"Yes, harnesser. Connect with her. You know the path to her soul," he heard in his mind as the old necromancer entered the circle with them.

She positioned herself behind Celine's back where he could see her. Scraggly hair lifted with energy and magic, and unbelievable power saturated the dome. "Touch her soul, Elijah. You can't fully harness her without embracing her soul completely. You know this. Your soul knows this."

"I can't," he gritted between clenched teeth.

"We can't hold this forever, and they will possess her once the shield folds. They will kill us all."

His gaze lifted to the demons. Hate glazed their faces, their eyes wholly focused on the woman in his arms. His power surged wildly, creating an impenetrable force. The tourmaline warmed against his skin, and the brand burned. His muscles rippled and bulged under the strain of this much energy.

Celine cried out against his chest and shook her head when the demons began screaming the chant in a unified voice.

"Now," the necromancer yelled.

Black wings exploded from his back. Ropes from his soul expanded from his body and thrust into Celine, seeking her soul, her heart, the very essence of who she was.

Slim arms squeezed his waist, and her face pressed against his chest. The ropes of his soul locked with hers, circled it, intertwined with it, bathing it in his energy. One strand pierced her heart and expanded in showers until he shielded her entire life force. Celine jerked in his arms, her soul reaching for his, the bond between them intensifying.

The demons shrieked and threw themselves at the barrier. A small area cracked and opened at the top, and they flooded in rapidly.

"You can't have her demons!" the necromancer shouted.

The corporeal bodies of the demons became one line of faces, circling them like a tornado, scratching at the barrier of his soul, but it was impenetrable.

Celine screamed and went slack against him.

The Druid dome collapsed.

The old necromancer lifted her arms and chanted in the ancient language. White light shot from her eyes, covering everyone and everything.

The demons shrieked one more time, fighting to remain before fading into nothing.

Celine's knees buckled, and he scooped her into his arms. His wings retracted, and the light faded.

"Inside, Elijah. Follow me. We need to talk."

"Where did they go?"

"To regroup, and when they return, you better remove any doubts. That wasn't a full harness. Secure your bond with her, or they will possess her."

His gaze dropped to the woman in his arms. She appeared young and frail, hauntingly beautiful. Everything was in place, but the harness wouldn't hold without the binds of love, and he couldn't love again.

Elijah didn't know what to do or think, except follow the necromancer inside the building. After pausing with her wrinkled hand on a panel in the wall, a section slid open to reveal a hidden elevator. She stepped inside, lifting one eyebrow when he didn't immediately join.

"There are levels to this building you know nothing of. Few do."

He turned sideways in order to maneuver into the small space with Celine cradled in his arms.

Once the doors closed, the necromancer faced him. "My name is Wilma."

"Wilma." Elijah let it roll off his tongue. "You don't look or sound like a Wilma."

Wilma grinned. "Better than old crone."

He chuckled out loud. "Well, Wilma. Where are we going?"

She lifted her cane and pointed at the woman in his arms. "Someplace where they can't find her."

"This book is burning my chest, so it has to be uncomfortable against her. Could you take it out and hold it?"

"No."

"Why the hell not?"

"It's spelled. Because you're her harnesser, it won't harm you."

Elijah dropped his head to the thick book poking from his shirt. "Crazy shit."

"Well, the shit's about to get deeper, harnesser."

"Wonderful," Elijah grumbled to the wall. His face tilted, studying Wilma. She was an odd little thing with her sharp mind but aged body. "What are you?"

"I'm Druidess."

"Witch?" he asked. "Isn't that the same thing?"

Her lips firmed. "No, it's not. Druidesses worship the Goddess Danu. Witches in this realm are mostly of light and earth, and they worship the Triple Goddess...The Maiden, The Mother, and The Crone. Dark witches summoned these demons and opened hell's door with black magic, thinking they could control it. You did us all a favor when you destroyed that coven."

"I'll miss those days."

"Why? Living off blood and the inability to tolerate sunlight? What a terrible curse."

"Yet your council cursed me with it, and you enacted it."

She waved one hand. "We'll get to that."

Elijah glanced at the ceiling before his gaze returned to the woman in his arms. Dark circles marred her porcelain skin, and she was light as a feather. Her sweats and t-shirt bagged off her frame, and her bare feet covered in cuts. Celine was too skinny for his taste, and guilt churned in his gut. He shouldn't have ignored the soul bond.

"She's been through much over the past week," Wilma commented.

"They destroyed her home. It resembled a war zone."

Celine's eyes twitched beneath her eyelids, and her muscles spasmed against his chest. "Is she dreaming?" He'd forgotten what it was like to dream. That was another part of his curse. No sleep.

"She communes with spirits even in sleep. Her power is strengthening."

"What about the demons?"

"She's harnessed to you, but not fully. They won't attempt to take her again tonight." Wilma's lips firmed. "This one is strong. Stronger than her mother."

"You knew her?"

"I trained her."

The elevator slowed to a stop, and the doors dinged before opening.

"Follow me, Elijah Drake."

Chapter 4

Celine strolled through a field of wildflowers that expanded for miles. Yellow daisies, roses, and tall grasses skimmed underneath her hands. Bright sunshine warmed her shoulders, and trees swayed in the soft breeze. A light floral scent filled her nostrils, and she inhaled deeply. It was a welcome sight after what she'd endured. She smiled when her mother waved from beneath a low-hanging tree branch in the distance, hurrying to meet her.

"I was worried about you," rushed out.

"I'm fine, but you must be careful, Celine. There are things you don't understand. Trust your harnesser. He'll never lead you astray."

She shook her head, thinking of Elijah. "I don't know him."

"I want to show you something, daughter. Come with me."

Celine followed her mother to a door that appeared from nowhere. Golden light emanated from the four seams. "What is this?"

"You've been summoned by the Druid Council."

"And this place? Why can't we stay here?"

"This field is similar to the first level of the Domain of Souls. Think of it as a waiting room."

Celine glanced at the door. "I don't want to go in there."

"Don't be afraid. The truth waits for you."

She reached for her mother's hand as the knob turned. In a whirl of blinding light, they stood in a room covered with Druid symbols and ancient writing. Men and women sat at a circular podium, and white hooded robes concealed their faces. "Where are we?"

"This is the Druid Council chamber. You're protected in these walls."

"Young Celine. We're honored to finally meet you," a deep male voice welcomed from the podium.

Celine glanced at her mother, but she was gone. "Mom?"

"Her spirit returned to where she belongs," one female answered.

Celine crossed her arms over her chest and bit the inside of her cheek. "Why am I here?"

"Your mother was one of us, a necromancer, and your father was a harnesser. Both were Unseelie. Did you know this?"

Celine nodded once. "I suspected."

"You're not a witch or medium or whatever this human world called you, Celine. You're a Druid necromancer, Queen of the House of Unseelie. And you're Fae. Elijah Drake is your harnesser."

"Is this why the coven in Salem wouldn't accept me?"

"Yes. They don't understand, and they fear what they can't control. The coven wasn't for you. Your harnesser eliminated it."

"What's a harnesser?" she asked the robe-shrouded figures, wishing she could see their faces.

"A harnesser keeps your soul out of harm's way. You have been entering the Domain of Souls without an anchor on this side, and that is how they followed you here. You became their portal or vessel. Do you understand what you've done?"

"I didn't mean to. This never happened before."

One of the council members smacked their palm against the podium, the sound echoing off the walls, startling her. "We don't tolerate excuses. You knew what you were doing and put everyone in harm's way with your recklessness. Your gifts aren't to be sold like common parlor tricks."

She wanted to hide, run, or wake up from this nightmare. This felt like a judgment and sentence. "I'm sorry. It was a way to earn a living. I've been branded an outcast. No one would give me a job after my mother's death, and my father disappeared. I'm alone."

"And for that reason, we'll grant you a chance to correct the error, Celine. You'll fix this now that your harnesser has risen."

"How? I don't know how?"

"You'll return to the Fae realm, where you'll learn under your harnesser and bond with him. The King of the Unseelie, your harnesser, has come into power."

"I'm not one of them. This world is all I've ever known."

Her eyes widened when one of the Druids rose from his seat and removed his hood. "We will dissolve the glamour to assist in the transition."

"Dad? Oh my God. Where have you been?" Celine stared at the man who resembled her father with noticeable changes. Druid symbols covered his pale skin like Elijah's. White hair fell to his shoulders, pointed ears rose on each side of his head, and his eyes glowed with the orange flames of a fire. She had only seen him as a human man. "Are you alive? Why did you leave?"

"I came with your mother for your transition, ascension, and journey. After you ascend, I'll return to your mother where I belong. We're a harnessed pair. We exist together."

"Ascension? Transition?"

"We concealed your Fae traits in order to blend with the human world. I was your mother's harnesser. I'm Unseelie or dark Fae. Your mother was an Unseelie necromancer. We can't be separated in life or death."

He removed the robe, and she gasped when black wings spread on either side of his body at least five feet. "This will be your true form, Celine, except for the wings. Only harnessers have wings. You're a necromancer and Queen of the Dark Unseelie. Use the gifts wisely and learn from your harnesser, Elijah Drake, King of the Unseelie. You'll burn in the light, and he'll consume the dark."

"I made a mess of everything. I don't know what I'm doing."

"You can commune with spirits, walk among the dead, and control them. Your fear is misplaced because you're untrained and for that, I apologize."

She moved three steps backward when he flew over the podium to land before her. Her memories of him were of an older man, a gentle man, not this powerful being with wings. "I'm sorry it had to be this way, Celine. We loved you more than you'll ever know. You'll understand once you bond with your harnesser."

He lifted one hand, palm open, offering a dull, irregular diamond. "This is your stone, the diamond of the Unseelie, rough and uncut. Put it somewhere safe. You'll need it."

Celine touched the stone with one finger before accepting it. "Why?"

Her father laid one hand on her shoulder. Her eyes lifted to his symbol-covered face. "Hell, and its demons. We've sealed the entrance from this end, so they've turned their attention to the Fae realm. You must protect our people by closing the doorway. You and the other queens. If they get in, they will destroy that world and have a way to enter this world."

"Why does it matter to them?"

"They are spirit, but we're physical bodies. They wish to live again. It would be unnatural to allow it to happen. They had their chance, and they chose wrong."

Celine dropped to her knees as symbols scorched and spread across her flesh. "What's happening?" she asked, panicked.

Pain encompassed her entire body. Pointed tips stretched the skin of her ears, and she cupped the sides of her head with her hands. A black wave encapsulated her flesh until no pink remained. Her eyes closed in a moan of agony, but they flashed open, burning with fire. She arched from the floor; her body wracked with convulsions. Knowledge filled her mind at a rapid pace, and she struggled to make sense of it all.

Her father walked in a circle around her writhing form. When the pain began to fade, he crouched before her and cupped her cheek. "Rest, daughter, then rise to claim your throne. You're the true mate to the Unseelie King."

Chapter 5

"Place her on my bed, Elijah."

Considering what haunted her, he was reluctant to lay her anywhere. She may have waged war with demonic forces, but her body bore the evidence of that battle. Silky, white hair trailed over his arm. His eyes tracked each scratch and bruise with rising anger. He laid her on the bed and pulled a quilt over her. She sighed in her sleep, one hand lifting over her head on the pillow.

"She's young and strong. Let her sleep. She'll recover."

"How old is she?" he asked, without turning away.

"Years aren't harmonious with wisdom," she quipped.

He snorted but left his sleeping necromancer to join Wilma by a small hearth with two rockers. Flames leaped to life with the wave of her hand, and the room warmed. Stones lined the small structure from top to bottom with Druid symbols carved into the surfaces. "What's this place?"

"We're deep in the ground below the council chamber."

"And you live here?"

Wilma leaned into her rocking chair with a sigh. "For too long. I look forward to my days in Danu's realm."

He hesitated, not wanting to deliver the bad news. "You know of Danu's passing?"

"I do, but her daughters will welcome me."

Elijah crossed one foot over his knee and placed the book in his lap. "So, why am I here besides harnessing Celine? And what's in this book?"

"Your kingdom is in chaos, and the Unseelie people are afraid. They need a king, not a spoiled brat with a grudge. We stripped all harnessers of the vampire curse."

"They've existed as vampires for years. Not fair or cool, Wilma, and I don't have a grudge. I'm full on pissed."

The corner of her mouth lifted in a smirk. "They'll survive. Swallow your pride, Elijah. Your queen needs you. She's not just a necromancer, but a time walker."

Elijah waved one hand before pinching the bridge of his nose. "This just gets better and better. Anything else?"

"Hell has found the cavern leading into the Fae realm, and the witches opened the door. You must seal it before they destroy that world, possess your queen, and come here. We've sealed the entrance from this side."

"Fucking perfect. I'm supposed to fix all that with an untrained necromancer?"

"You'll guide her."

He opened the book in his lap, scanning the contents. "With this, I suppose?"

"Yes. And your heart."

His eyes lifted from the book. "My heart died with Laura."

"You lie. I was in the Druid dome with you. I saw the connection to Celine with my own eyes."

"You hallucinated, hag. Have you been smoking some of that magical marijuana in here?"

Wilma cackled, rocking back and forth. "She wasn't what you thought."

"Who?"

"Laura."

The book snapped closed. "Enlighten me."

"Demon."

Elijah rose from his chair. "This conversation is over."

Wilma waved one hand, forcing him back into the seat. "Listen to me and listen well. There will come a time when you're forced to choose. Look with your harnesser eyes, not with your heart. Always see the soul first. Don't forget your training, Elijah."

His face tilted. "I told you my heart is dead. I don't want to be with her or care for her. You forced me into this."

Wilma snapped her cane against the stone. "Lies. All lies. You know how the soul bond works."

His head lifted to the ceiling when dust trailed in a single line and jumped to his feet when the space vibrated. "I thought they couldn't find her here."

"It's time to go," Wilma whispered, making no move to rise from her rocking chair. "I'll handle the demons left on this side."

*****

Celine's eyes snapped open in an unfamiliar room. Voices drifted from somewhere close. She recognized Elijah's, but not the female.

She squinted at the stone ceiling, listening to every word of their conversation. Her heart constricted. He may have saved her, but he didn't want her. Tears burned her eyes, but she pushed the hurt deep down with the rest. *Unwanted* was something she was used to.

If he didn't want to be with her, that was fine. She wouldn't force him. The transformation came with knowledge. She knew him, his history, all about the Fae realm, and what she was. Not every queen required a king.

The room vibrated as she rose from the bed and tossed the patchwork quilt aside. The demons were back, struggling to find her. They circled above the building, waiting for her to emerge. Her eyes narrowed on the ceiling. Strength and power filled her body when she used to feel weak. She stretched her legs, grimacing at the Druid marks on her flesh. She lifted her hands, frowning at the symbols, and touched her pointed ears. Elijah had them too, but it didn't matter. She didn't need his protection any longer.

With a thought, black pants and a tunic formed to replace her ratty clothes. A portal established into Fae beside the bed. The door jerked open, and Elijah stormed into the room. Their gazes locked, but his widened on the portal.

"Don't," he warned.

With a smirk, she stepped inside and exited within the Fae realm. At once, her senses expanded on high alert. Strange scents and fantastical images overwhelmed her mind, and she crouched on the ground to absorb this new world. Tall grasses swayed back and forth. Enormous trees reached for the stars overhead, and the tinkling of water was nearby. Her gaze lifted to the twin purple moons.

She inhaled a deep breath, slowly rising from her concealed position, walking without a destination in mind. The Druid Council implanted the knowledge in her mind, but it didn't come with a map. She entered the Fae realm to get away from Elijah and the demons. It wasn't like she could return home.

At the edge of a vast forest, she halted, peering into the unfamiliar place. Gnarled trees seemed to move in the moonlight, and she thought she saw eyes peeping from bushes. Celine glanced over her shoulder when laughter from a female voice reached her ears. She pivoted, studying the two newcomers with interest. One had light blonde hair, and the other was dark headed with pointy ears like her. They smiled and waved as they approached.

Celine stepped backward, unsure and edgy. Her muscles tensed, preparing to run when one yelled, "Don't go. We mean you no harm."

The dark headed one smiled. "Don't be afraid. I'm Nena, Queen of the Fae and this is Stevie, Queen of the Lycan. Stevie saw you in a dream. We've been waiting for you."

The concept seemed preposterous, but then everything seemed crazy right now. "What do you want?"

The pair stopped several feet from her position, close enough to view their beautiful faces, but far enough away not to invade her personal space. "We've come to welcome you and help you."

"Why would you do that?"

Nena and Stevie glanced at each other. "Because we were once where you are."

"Elijah is a dick. I don't want him. I hope you're not here to convince me otherwise."

The women burst into laughter.

Celine watched the pair with curiosity. "What's so funny?"

Stevie grinned from ear to ear, her face lighting with humor. "Dagen, my mate, chained me to a wall."

Nena tucked her hair behind her pointy ear. "Tristan hounded me."

The two women looked at each other before Nena smiled again, sliding one hand over her stomach. "I've met Elijah, and he is a dick. He has a heart buried under all his bullshit, though."

Celine snorted, but her gaze dropped to Nena's stomach. "You're pregnant."

Nena winked and glanced at her tummy. "Is that what this is?"

Celine's lips twitched, trying not to smile. "You two are stunning. Look at me. Branded with symbols." She huffed in annoyance. "Elijah said his heart is dead, and he doesn't want to be with me, so I left him. I don't need a king."

"Good for you," Stevie praised.

When Stevie held up one hand, Celine's eyes narrowed. "You have symbols too? You're Druid?"

"I am," Stevie answered. "You're beautiful, Celine. Different isn't ugly."

"Why don't you come stay with me at the Fae castle?" Nena offered. "I'd love to have another woman in that monstrosity."

Everyone gasped when Elijah snorted, emerging from the forest behind Celine. He banded her waist with both arms and yanked her against him. "That won't be necessary, ladies."

Nena tilted her head. "You don't seem as pale, Elijah. Are you feeling well?"

Celine cringed at the teasing remark.

"Don't like my new look, Queen of the Fae?" he slurred.

Celine grinned at Nena and Stevie but held her tongue.

Stevie winked at her and lifted her chin to Elijah. "I've sensed you stalking at night, and now we'll have to deal with you in daylight. Buy some sunblock since your pasty skin hasn't seen the light of day for how long?"

Elijah chuckled. "Are you insinuating I'm old?"

Nena tapped one finger against her lips. "I think there's some gray in that white hair."

Celine tried not to laugh, but couldn't stop it from escaping.

"You think that's funny, mate?" he growled in her ear.

"The word mate implies mating which hasn't occurred," she quickly retorted over her shoulder. "And won't."

"Cock-blocked," Nena teased.

"Oh, I like you a lot, Celine," Stevie said with a twinkle in her eyes.

Elijah chuckled at Stevie, his breath warming her ear. "You shouldn't fuck in the open, Queen of the Lycan. Never know who's watching."

Stevie gasped. "And you shouldn't spy on people."

"Nice ass for a lady with a baby."

"I hate you," Stevie hissed. "Wait till Dagen finds out."

"That big fluff ball?" Elijah teased. "He's too busy chasing you."

Stevie grinned and bristled. "So hot."

Nena snorted, watching Elijah and Stevie trade jabs. "Ignore them, Celine. They're both perverts."

"Like you and Tristan? Let's fill Celine in on your secret, Nena." Elijah taunted.

Nena's eyes widened. "Don't you dare."

Stevie laughed.

Elijah's chest rumbled against her back, and she shivered with him this close.

Her two new friends gave her a bit of courage. "I would prefer to stay with Nena at her castle."

"Well, I don't care what the fuck you'd like," Elijah grumbled, opened a portal, and shoved her through.

*****

Celine turned on him with flames burning her eyes. "Ever heard of the word gentleman?"

"Fucking blasphemy," he yelled. "I haven't been a gentleman in years and don't plan to start anytime soon."

"Profanity insinuates a lack of intelligence and imagination," she shouted at him.

He jerked back, surprised. "Are you calling me dumb?"

"Dumb, crude, idiotic, bossy, and pushy. The list of attributes grows by the second."

He circled her petiteness, noticing the rise and fall of her chest, the way her pulse throbbed in her neck, the pointed ears, and the symbols carved into her skin. "I should've left you to those demons."

She frowned but didn't flinch when he stopped directly in front of her, towering over her and crowding her body. One finger poked his chest, and he almost laughed. Her chin lifted. "I can't believe I've been saddled with you as a mate. You don't even want me, and I definitely don't want you."

"Fucking lies. All lies. You were content to cuddle against my chest and wrap those slender arms around my neck when I found you. Even now your body says you want me. It's the way of mates."

Her nostrils flared, so he moved even closer, inhaling her sweet breath. She licked her bottom lip and placed her hands on the curvature of her hips. Her gaze slid over his face with an expression of disgust, and his body instantly hardened in response. "No retort, Celine?"

"I thought you would be different. We may be mates, but I don't want you," she hissed.

He leaned enough that his lips hovered over hers, barely an inch separating them. "More lies? I attached my soul to yours. I know you want me, and I can't wait to fuck you. At least I'm honest about it."

"Acting on basic lust shows a lack of discipline, Elijah."

"You're scolding me? Seriously? I can fuck four women at once or walk away."

"Disgusting," she yelled.

"Why? Because I'm confident?"

"No. Because you're so bitter. The connection runs both ways. You hate that you have to assume responsibility for your ignored kingdom, for me, and for the decisions you made. You're a spoiled child throwing a tantrum."

Her words cut deep, too deep. And when she backed four steps away, he experienced the loss in waves. Her eyes may be flames, but she was hurt and afraid. "How old are you, Celine?"

"Twenty-two."

He rose to his full height to glare at her and crossed his arms over his chest. "You know nothing about me."

"I've seen enough, and I don't want to remain where I'm not wanted. I'll stay in this place until I send the demons back where they came from."

"I'm the only one who can train and protect you, Celine."

"Not true," a deep voice spoke, emerging from the trees.

Elijah's gaze flicked to the one called Jax, and his eyebrow twitched. "Wake from your nap, sleeping beauty?"

Jax smiled. "I did as you can see, and I've come to help our newcomer. It's a pleasure to meet you, Celine. I'm Druid of old."

Elijah wanted to rip Jax's head off when he bowed before his mate and snorted when Celine smiled in return.

"You're not a harnesser," Elijah practically growled. "Shouldn't you be with Stevie?"

"True, but I'm Druid and can assist with your mate's training. Wilma sent me. I plan to visit with Stevie after I leave here. Thank you for your concern."

"You can't protect her in the Domain of Souls."

"You're right. We'll need you for that," Jax stated.

Elijah lifted one eyebrow. "Fucking hell. I've been reduced to prostitute for harnessing."

Celine maneuvered beside Jax, touching his arm. Elijah thought his head might explode.

"I think it's perfect," she beamed. "May I have my mother's book?"

"No, you may not."

*****

He didn't want to be with her, said his heart was dead, and refused to play nice, so he had no reason to act this way. Jax was the perfect solution. "Why?"

"Because I haven't gone through it yet."

She glanced at Jax, her handsome teacher. He was a gorgeous man, with dark hair and hard muscles. And he didn't hate her like the mate she'd been attached to at the hip. "Any suggestions?"

Jax grinned from ear to ear, glancing between her and Elijah. "When you're ready, give me a shout."

"And how am I to do that?" Celine asked, exasperated.

Jax nodded to Elijah. "He knows how."

Celine threw both hands in the air. "Unbelievable. Elijah doesn't want me here, and you're abandoning me."

Jax reached for her hand, but Elijah snarled with a low growl.

"And why are you growling like some wild animal?" she demanded, turning on Elijah.

"It's okay, Celine. Don't worry about it. Call me when you're ready, and Elijah is ready."

With both hands on her hips, Celine glared at Elijah after Jax disappeared. At this angle, it was the first time she noticed the gloomy structure behind him in the woods. "Is that my new home? Or my dungeon?"

Elijah's full lips lifted in an almost smile, and her stomach turned over. She didn't understand her fluctuating responses to him.

"Depends on that mouth."

His annoying tone grated on her nerves. "Well, where are your loyal subjects, great Unseelie King?"

"Ran off to greener pastures, I suspect."

"It's ugly," she observed, tilting her head.

"At least it doesn't have demons crawling all over it."

She bristled, narrowed her eyes, and imagined committing bodily harm to this man. "That was a mistake."

"Fucking cheap carnival tricks. You should know better than to sell your gift for a few bucks."

"I was alone, with no way to support myself. That cheap trick paid the bills."

"Whatever."

"I didn't know I was a version of Fae, I didn't know I needed a harnesser, and I didn't know I belonged in this drab place," she yelled. "Better than sucking blood."

"Yes, blood. I quite enjoyed my cursed time as a vampire. Now I have no harem of blood slaves, and I'm stuck with the queen of the demons."

"Fuck you, Elijah." The words had barely left her mouth when she covered it with one hand.

Elijah snorted and chuckled, pointing at her. "Best day ever to see you lose your shit. What were those insults you tossed out earlier? Lack of imagination and intelligence?"

Her temper exploded, and she attacked him. He laughed harder when she plowed into his stomach. They rolled onto the ground, but she didn't know if it was from her or him. She suspected him. It didn't matter, though. Her anger never reached this level one time with anyone. Her knee landed in his ribs, and her fist on his sculpted jaw.

He rolled her over, his body straddled on her stomach. "Hot. This is fucking hot, Celine."

She lifted her knee, contacting his balls. He slipped off, moaning about crazy bitches, cupping his crotch, but he still smiled. "They're still alive, baby," he chuckled.

"I'm not your baby, Elijah," she grumbled, straddling him again. He tried to grab her at the waist, but she pushed his hands to either side of his head. "The dark Unseelie King defeated," she teased, trying not to gloat.

"Your tits are in my face, Celine. If you slide on up, I'll eat your pussy."

"You're such a dick."

He licked his lips. "Well, now that I think about it, my dick is hard. How's that monster feel between your legs?"

He was impossible. Her eyes lowered to his. "Definitely not monstrous."

A shitty grin spread across his lips. "I'm the only one allowed to lie in this relationship."

"Is this a relationship? I must've misunderstood because I thought it was more of a hostage situation."

"Sizzling fucking hot, Celine. I like hostage situations, especially with attitude-laden women. Give me what you gave me on the dance floor."

"Error in judgment."

"I don't think so, mate. You feel the draw as much as I do. The sooner you accept it and act on it, the happier you'll be."

"You don't want me like that, and I don't want you," she stated, climbing off him.

Celine stomped toward the dilapidated structure with a frown, massaging her hand. Vines covered the tarnished stone, but it rose three stories from the ground with grimy windows lining the front. Statues of gargoyles faced and glared at anyone daring to stroll through the black iron gate. Barren shrubs and wilting trees surrounded the property, but there was a small stream to the right. The dark forest appeared poised to swallow it at any moment, and the night sky didn't do it any justice.

Elijah's arms circled her waist, and he yanked her against his chest. She bit her lip in surprise. "What and why? And can't you be gentle?"

He chuckled beside her cheek. "There's nothing gentle about me, Celine. Don't try to change me."

Her eyes lowered to his hand, stroking hers. Tender but dominant, Elijah's aggressive nature was the one thing she liked about him. There's no way she'd ever tell him. He had a habit of surprising her, knocking her off guard, and causing her head to spin. Who knew she'd adore an aggressive man? Maybe it was the bond? Or perhaps her own nature? She was Unseelie, after all. A devious grin lifted the corners of her mouth. Either way, she couldn't get enough of it, and that made him dangerous and her reckless.

"First lesson," he breathed close to her ear, lifting her sore hand and licking it.

His body pressed to her back, his dick curving into her ass, and she hated herself for the heat simmering in her veins. "Stop it, Elijah. Go on with the lesson and stop acting like you care."

"Why would you think I don't care?" he teased, sliding his tongue between her knuckles.

Shivers slithered over her spine, straight to her sex, and her lips firmed. He toyed with her emotions, her attraction to him, knowing the bond couldn't be stopped.

"Fae are magical beings. You're more than a necromancer, Celine. Envision your new home as you wish it to be."

His tongue swirled on her wrist.

"Impossible." Trying to focus became difficult.

"Nothing is impossible, Celine. Your mind limits you," he barely whispered, kissing each finger.

She shuddered when his breath warmed her ear and neck, and pieces of his hair fell over her shoulder.

"Cold?"

"No. Well, maybe a little." She wasn't cold. She was on fire.

Her eyes rolled to the night sky, and she jerked her hand away, crossing her arms over her stomach. He pressed even closer, his dick snug against the crease of her ass, and his hands covering her bare arms.

"Better?"

She could only nod her head. The urge to turn into him and bury her face in his chest was suffocating. She'd been alone too long, with no comfort or anyone to lean on. It was exhausting carrying the weight of everything on her shoulders. This man, the caring man, was the one she found difficult to ignore, even if it was a lie.

"Focus, Celine."

Deep and hypnotic, his voice stirred something deep in the pit of her stomach. Her eyes snapped open when he cupped her hand, warm fingers sliding back and forth, and the other hand trickled across her upper chest.

"Feel me. Feel the earth. Inhale the crisp night air deep into your lungs. Allow your senses to expand and grasp onto the magic that feeds your body. It's your lifeline when all else fails. The magic of the Fae dwells in us. It's everywhere. All we have to do is tap into the thread."

"I don't know if I can, Elijah."

"You can. Give the Unseelie a reason to believe, and a reason to come home."

"I'm afraid." And she was as black light particles swirled, and the ground trembled. Her king, her mate, coaxed her magic by seduction, refusing to allow her to cower.

"I'm with you now and always."

Her head rested against his chest, and her eyes closed. She couldn't fight him or the magnetic force he wielded. A sigh left her lips, and her magic burst from her soul.

*****

Oh, damn. His little necromancer was smoking hot, and possessed a naughty side, driving him to press for more. He grinned above her head, sliding his dick against her ass. Her breasts lifted with her deep inhales, and goosebumps covered her arms. She wasn't immune to him, and the soul bond only made it worse. Focus, he reminded himself.

Years had passed since he experienced this, and he absorbed as much as he could as fast as he could along with her delicious scent. The vampire curse stripped him of almost everything except the animalistic need for blood and the ability to open portals, but it didn't strip him of desire for a true mate. And his necromancer melted like sweet sugar on his tongue.

Fae magic, Unseelie magic, was potent and powerful, laced with an undercurrent of all Fae in existence. And the woman in his arms possessed more than most. She just didn't know it yet and didn't know how to use it.

The moment she succumbed to what she felt instead of what she knew, a funnel of magic surrounded them. Her muscles tightened at first but relaxed into the energy and into him. No longer did she slump forward in his hold, but curved into him as she embraced pure magic in its truest form. Power swelled, and they both held it in, riding the current of energy. His dick throbbed against her tight ass. How easy it would be to yank her pants down and fuck her right here with the magic fueling every sensation. The bond called to him, so he knew it called to her. He inhaled a deep breath, releasing it slowly.

"Now focus on the house, Celine. Light it up, sexy."

Their connection was strong, unbreakable, and the harnesser in him rose with her. The symbols on their flesh glowed as threads of white magic expanded from his soul to join the black light particles. Several of his strands pierced her flesh, combining with her soul, and she welcomed him without hesitation.

In this state, they were one. They were Unseelie, necromancer and harnesser, king and queen, and fated mates.

Her breath quickened, their soul bond strengthening. His nostrils flared with her scent, and his dick swelled against her tight little ass. He needed to bond with her, and he needed it now. A surge of energy erupted in waves, and he flinched with a grin spreading.

In a brilliant flash, magic encapsulated the house from top to bottom and spread over the land surrounding it. Blood-red roses sprouted from the shrubs, and green leaves thrust from the thorny stems. The old stones in the house glimmered with metallic shards under the moonlight, and the dingy windows became shiny new. The vines covering the home rustled and turned bright green and black. Dark purple clematis-like blooms opened on the vines.

Dragons roared overhead, and creatures he hadn't seen in years emerged from the forest. Ogres, dark fairies, and hairy beasts watched in awe. Giant bats circled above, and mutant butterflies landed on the petals of the rose and clematis blooms.

A mighty rush of water filled the stream, and the forest beyond breathed a sigh of relief with red, black, and gray leaves. Fireflies lifted from the grasses to circle the trees.

Gargoyle statues cracked and stretched for the first time in years. Their wings expanded, and they took to the sky to join the dragons.

Celine turned in his arms. Orange flames filled her eyes, laced with desire. She laid one palm over his chest, the tourmaline burning between them, and the other hand gripped his biceps. Her hair rose from her shoulders, and her breasts lifted. Confident and seductive, this was a powerful necromancer in all her glory.

Elijah inhaled a deep breath as creatures screeched to the moons with their freedom. The Unseelie kingdom lived. This was his home and his queen.

Their mouths met in a tempest of power. Magic flared wildly and pulsated with the first swipes of their tongues. Her unique taste filled his mouth, and he groaned under the lustful kiss. The essence of the richest blood couldn't compare to the taste of Celine, and he wanted everything.

Small breasts pressed against his chest. One of his hands slid along her spine to cup her neck and bend her to his dominance. There was no resistance as she sighed into his mouth.

"You said you would love me forever."

Elijah jerked at Laura's voice. The magic dissipated when he backed away from Celine, still licking his lips. It wasn't possible to hear Laura here. A woman's scream split the night, and he turned to face the forest.

"What is that?" Celine asked, pointing toward the tree line.

Elijah's eyes narrowed on the form of a woman, ethereal and beautiful, black hair flowing out behind her. She floated between the trees, emerging from the forest with a sinister smirk. A black gown brushed against her shins, and her feet were bare.

"Demon," Celine hissed. "You're not welcome here."

"I'll rule when I possess your body, Queen of the Unseelie," she wailed. "This will be mine."

Elijah could only watch as his queen gripped her tourmaline, lifted her free hand, and funneled her magic directly at Laura.

With unnatural twitching and moans of agony, Laura departed the realm in a fog of black smoke.

Celine confronted him with flames encompassing her eye sockets, but for a different reason. "You better start talking, my king."

*****

Wilma's words haunted him. She'd warned him, but he refused to believe Laura was a demon until now. He pinched the bridge of his nose, trying to recall the conversation.

Wilma cackled, rocking back and forth. "She wasn't what you thought."

"Who?"

"Laura."

The book snapped closed. "Then enlighten me."

"Demon."

Celine touched his arm, and his gaze fell on her worried face. "Talk to me, Elijah."

But he didn't know what to say.

"Ghost?" Celine asked.

"I think so. Maybe. Let's go inside, and I'll tell you everything."

Celine gestured to their audience. "What about them?"

Expectant faces, hopeful faces, stared at him. A deep sigh rose from his chest. He couldn't ignore them or abandon them again. "Welcome home, Unseelie."

Their gazes pivoted to Celine, and he tucked her close to his side. "This is Celine. I've found your queen. She's a necromancer."

One ogre stepped closer. He was huge, bald, and as ugly as they came, but he dropped to one knee. "Welcome Queen Celine."

Celine trembled at his side, yet her chin lifted. She hesitantly moved away from him to approach the ogre with his head bowed. "What's your name?"

The ogre lifted his face. "Hogden."

Elijah watched with pride swelling in his chest as Celine touched the beast's shoulder with one hand. "There's no need to bow, Hogden. I'm one of you."

When Hogden smiled, revealing his decaying teeth, Elijah grimaced and chuckled out loud. The ogre rose from the ground to tower over his mate's much smaller frame, but she still showed no fear. Instead, she sidestepped him to greet the others. "Welcome," she said, touching each one.

It was a bitter pill to swallow, realizing you were wrong about so many things. Laura's appearance shocked and shattered the bitterness he'd held onto for so long. His lips twitched. He had to find a way to bridge the gap and bond with Celine.

"Your curse is gone?"

His attention swiveled on the tiny fairy buzzing before him, and he nodded once. "I'm no longer a vampire."

Her tiny face tilted, studying him.

"Don't fear me, Elisa of the Dark Fairies."

A breathtaking smile spread across her little face, and she motioned toward the rose bushes. Hundreds of dark fairies buzzed and circled him.

"My queen would be most gracious if you tended to her thorny roses," he offered to the swarm.

"We would be honored, King of the Unseelie," Elisa answered.

He laughed when the swarm of dark fairies circled him before returning to the roses. It was the first time he'd genuinely laughed in years.

Upon Celine's approach, he studied her with fresh eyes. He was wrong to be cruel when she'd done nothing to deserve it.

"The ogres have agreed to be protectors of the forest, and the rest are happy to not live in fear anymore of the wicked vampire with a bad attitude."

Elijah pretended to be offended. "I don't have a bad attitude."

Her eyebrows arched, so he bent at the waist to look directly into her eyes. "There's not one fucking thing wrong with me."

"There he is."

"Who?"

"The foul-mouthed king."

"I gave up blood. It's too much to relinquish my extensive vocabulary. It's one of my finer qualities."

"You're so full of yourself. And live to be annoying."

Elijah snapped his teeth together. "Damn straight."

Celine glanced at the refurbished house. "You going to give me the grand tour?"

He gestured toward the gate. "Lead the way. I'm eager to see if you used pink?"

"Pink everything right down to the sheets on your bed."

He deliberately slid his gaze from the top of her head to her feet. "Our bed."

"I don't think so." Her mouth firmed, the lips he'd just kissed and still tasted on his tongue, denying him.

Elijah backed toward the house with a sly grin. "Think again."

*****

Celine followed behind, admiring the wide set of Elijah's shoulders, narrow waist, thick legs, and firm backside. She remembered every delicious detail of his body when they danced, and when he helped her. He could be nasty or considerate, and those switched within a millisecond. He was a complete stranger, a wild beast always on the hunt, yet she wasn't afraid of him. It was frustrating to feel these things and not act on them.

White hair swayed against the black shirt, and his fathomless eyes revealed authentic emotion if you knew how to look. He was a big man, moving with confidence and ease.

Wicked and sensual, he made her feel wanted with that display of magic. And that connection was addictive. The kiss left a stamp on her soul, and she needed more. Every cell in her body cried out to be close to him, but not with him attached to another woman.

He strolled nonchalantly, gazing at the changes, and even plucked a bloom from a rosebush. Long fingers twirled the rose, and he brought it to his nose, lost in his thoughts. This was a different man, a content man, and she liked him this way. He oozed sexuality, drawing her on a raw feral level she'd never experienced with anyone.

The fairies swirled her waist, disappearing inside a blood red rose shrub. Sharp thorns protruded from the stem, but she couldn't stop herself from caressing a bloom. "Ouch," she gasped when a thorn stuck in her forefinger.

"Let me see," Elijah crooned, pulling the digit to his lips. "There's tiny thorns in the blooms as well."

She almost sighed when he touched her fingertip to his mouth, sliding it over the plump flesh. He sucked the drop of blood from the tip, and she gulped, staring when he used his teeth to withdraw the thorn.

"Yum. Blood still tastes divine."

"Nasty," she scoffed, her eyes rolling to the sky. He ruined the moment.

"Should I carry you over the threshold?"

She paused when his eyebrow arched, something dangerous filtering into the black void of his eyes. "No. That won't be necessary."

A lazy, sexy smile lifted the corners of his mouth, and her stomach somersaulted. He pushed the door open and paused in the foyer. "You didn't change anything."

"It's yours. Why would I change your home? Besides, it's not like you want me here."

"There's much you don't understand. We need to have a discussion. Follow me."

It shocked her he would voluntarily share anything or be civil about it.

The interior of his home was clean and somewhat beautiful. Oil paintings hung on the wall of a man and woman Elijah resembled, scenic landscapes, and many sharp swords. The home definitely had a masculine feel to it, with blues and grays dominating much of the décor. He led her past several iron doors before halting at one and withdrawing a set of old keys from a hallway table. The door swung inward, and he gestured for her to enter.

"Amazing," she exclaimed. Full bookshelves rose at least forty feet against white walls. Globes and trinkets decorated small tables, he had positioned two couches in front of a wall of windows, and a small hearth occupied the middle.

What she assumed was his desk dominated the opposite side of the room, with papers and books covering it. She didn't think he'd show his private office to her, but Elijah surprised her again, knocking her off balance as seemed to be his way.

Celine strode to the desk, one finger sliding over many of his possessions, but jerked it away when he cleared his throat behind her. She glanced over her shoulder to where he waited with arms crossed and booted feet spread shoulder width apart. "Sorry. Just curious."

"Go ahead," he said, nodding toward the desk.

"It's not my business."

"Your mother's book is there. I haven't had time to open it yet."

"Is this another lesson?"

Elijah's face tilted, but he moved to the desk and sat in the chair. "Come here."

Celine positioned herself so she could look over his shoulder. Carefully, he opened the book. She'd seen it many times, tried to study it, but didn't understand much of it. The symbols were foreign and much of the writing scribbled and illegible.

"This speaks of the Domain of Souls and the different levels, but you've already been there."

"Yes, and don't care to return."

He turned the pages, reading her mother's words, occasionally pausing until he found what he wanted. "Here we go. You're a necromancer, born from harnesser and necromancer. You banished Laura from this realm. I didn't understand how until now."

"What do you mean?"

"Some necromancers are so powerful they can reanimate the dead, enslave them, or banish them. You grabbed your talisman at the same moment you confronted Laura. You didn't know you were doing it because you hadn't been properly trained. And in the club, spirits flocked to you. They hovered above our heads, but they were there."

"I touched it frequently when in the Domain of Souls."

"Because it channels your magic."

"Channel? I don't understand."

"Focuses it. When we fixed this place, the magic went everywhere at once, but when you focused on Laura, you banished her."

"How did she even get here?"

"That's a significant question. The Druid Council said there was a portal here, an opening that we need to close or block. Maybe she traveled through it."

"Where is it, and why haven't more come through?"

"Another good question I don't have an answer to."

"We have to find it. Like now."

Elijah turned his chair, grabbed her by the waist, and sat her on his lap. "We will."

A bit surprised, she tried to rise, but he wouldn't let her. "What are you doing?"

*****

He didn't want to broach the subject, but she needed to know everything. And he didn't like her so far from him. "Laura."

Her eyes narrowed before dropping to her clasped hands. "You loved her, right? I heard you loud and clear."

"I did. At least, I thought I did. Have you ever been in love, Celine?"

"I dated. There was one guy I thought could be something special, but we grew apart when he went to college. Our priorities changed. I cried for days over him."

"New love is powerful love. Would you agree?"

"Yes."

"But that doesn't mean it's everlasting or real. Laura and I met when I was at the Druid Council. She wasn't Fae. I was there with my father for training and loved roaming the city in my free time. Laura worked at a coffee shop, and I'm a sucker for great coffee. We had an instant attraction and began meeting in secret. The council warned me not to get involved with humans, that a harnesser always has a necromancer, and that it would end badly for her."

Celine finally lifted her eyes to his.

"I shared things with her I shouldn't, and she was eager to listen. She became obsessed with my harnesser talents, started messing with ghost hunting, and dabbling in dark witchcraft. I harnessed her when she went too far. It was like a game for her."

"I don't understand."

"She was involved with a group who would willingly harm themselves to cross to the other side. They were ravenous for information on spirits and what happens after death."

"That's insane. The spirits aren't to be toyed with. They invite. You don't barge your way into the Domain of Souls. And harming yourself?"

"My point exactly. I begged her to stop, but one night she went too far. She crossed over without informing me. I tried to bring her back but couldn't find her. I don't even know that I could. The connection wasn't right and never was."

"Why?"

"I thought we were in love, but the council was correct. It was an immature love. We weren't soulmates. She was human, and I was an Unseelie Fae and harnesser. The council said Laura had manipulated me, that her group had been on their radar for years, but I refused to listen. My punishment was vampirism, and that curse wasn't lifted until you came along."

"How did they know?"

"The Druid Council are powerful. They can sense the slightest magic, good or evil. Bianca, Danu's daughter, approached me. She only said my harnesser talents were needed, but once I arrived at the Druid Council, I left pissed and confused. What I thought was love wasn't love at all. Bianca gave me a talisman that matched yours. As soon as I touched it, I connected to you. That only happens between mated pairs."

"But you still love Laura. I saw it in your eyes, Elijah. I can't be your mate with a ghost haunting you."

"I was shocked. That's what you saw."

"And now?"

Elijah toyed with the chain and black tourmaline suspended from her neck. "Now I know I have a mate in this life."

"She said she would possess me."

His eyes narrowed on the tourmaline. "She can't because you're bound to me. I'm your harnesser."

"The old woman said we weren't bound completely. I remember my parents. The love between them was unbelievable, and everyone felt it." Celine laid one hand over his heart. "You're not mine. Not like that. The instant Laura spoke to you, our connection broke."

What could he say? It was true, but not for the reason Celine assumed. She was wrong. He didn't still love Laura. He regretted everything that happened and was filled with guilt, but the woman on his lap was the one he wanted. That was the truth he accepted.

She licked her lips, and he tracked the slide of her tongue. Her palm was warm against his chest, and her ass snug against his groin. "Bind with me, Celine."

"No." She pushed against his chest, but he didn't miss the disappointment on her features.

"Why?"

Hurt eyes met his. "Because I want more, I expect more, and I deserve more."

He didn't stop her when she rose from his lap, but laid one hand over hers, preventing her from darting away. "Human emotion isn't the same as binding between mates. You want fucking prince charming on a magic carpet? Words of love? That's not me, but I'll have you."

She jerked her hand from beneath his. "Not like this, you won't."

*****

Why did he have to ruin everything?

Celine put distance between them, keenly aware of his presence. Elijah couldn't be trusted, and she couldn't trust herself where he was concerned.

"It was you on the dance floor that night."

His eyes lowered. "Yes. I was there."

"Why?"

"The tourmaline and the bond led me to you."

"Who were the couples outside that shielded us?"

"Harnessed pairs."

"I see. Did the council force you to help me?"

"They did, and I tried to fight it, but our bond was too tight. I fought a losing battle."

"Do you even find me attractive, Elijah? Or is it just a spell?"

"Our souls bonded as mates, but I also find you ridiculously sexy, especially those dark eyes. And your body was created for wicked things like my mouth."

She chuckled to herself. If he only knew the wicked thoughts in her mind. There were layers to Elijah. He could be a complete dick, turn the tables in an instant, and be sexy sweet. What made him tick? What was he like before?

She bit the inside of her cheek, spinning a globe on the sofa table. "What happened to your parents? I'm assuming those were their portraits in the hall."

Elijah leaned in his chair and propped his feet on his desk. "The prior king had them assassinated."

"Prior king?"

His fingers linked over his taut abdomen as he watched every movement she made. It was unnerving and thrilling, to say the least.

"King Tristan's father was an asshole. He killed everyone he perceived a threat or hunted them until they left."

"King Tristan?"

"The Fae King. This is the land of the Fae. There are several factions who live here...dragons, Lycan,

Unseelie, and Fae, as well as fairies, ogres, many magical creatures."

"And everyone gets along?"

His eyebrow lifted as a broad grin spread. "It's a fucking utopia."

She rolled her eyes to the ceiling and snorted. "Utopia? People talk about it, but I don't believe in it."

"Why?"

"Necromancer and all that. I never fit in anywhere."

"But you found a way."

"I survived by learning to keep my mouth shut. People rarely want the truth they seek."

"What happened to your parents, Celine?"

Memories haunted her from that time, and her gaze lifted to the windows surrounding the fireplace. "My Mom became distant, distracted, and said they wouldn't leave her alone. Physical symptoms manifested. It became a struggle just to get her to eat until she finally refused. It was a heartbreaking tragedy to watch, but I understand better now. You know, she appeared right before you arrived. I'll never forget it. She said there was a time to fight and a time to run, and I should run. She's appeared several times and always when I'm in trouble."

"Demons can wreak havoc on the mind, even the strongest."

Celine withdrew a book from the case and opened it. "Divination?"

He nodded once. "I've had a long time to study. Your father?"

She snapped the book closed and returned it to its place on the shelf. "Now that I know about you, what you are, and what I am, I think he chose to join her. He even said as much when I transitioned."

Elijah's face tilted. "And they never told you before?"

One hand slid across the fireplace mantle, fingers flicking the unique stones he used for decoration. Rose quartz, amethyst, hematite, and sunstone twinkled in the light. "They hinted. Mom began my training at age sixteen. Simple lessons like how to make the connection, the levels of the Domain of Souls, and astral projection. One day she stopped, refusing to teach me anything else. She became obsessed over the book and spent hours locked in the study."

"What did your father say?"

"He told me to give her time. Once, he caught me with her book and jerked it from my hands. He warned me to never open it again, and I didn't. I thought about it, even opened it a few times in secret, but the words made no sense."

Elijah grabbed the book and positioned it on his lap.

"You shouldn't, Elijah. I'm afraid for you."

His gaze lifted to hers. "Damn. No one has ever said that."

She swallowed hard as a sexy smile spread across his mouth. When his attention returned to the book, she released the breath she held.

He flipped to the last few entries, then tossed it on his desk with a growl. "That's not your mother's handwriting. That's demonic writing."

"What?"

"Your mother was being haunted by demons, just as you are."

"Why?"

"Wilma said you were a time walker and necromancer."

Celine stopped before his desk and braced both hands on the wood. "And if I can time walk, then a demon could prevent their death. A chance to live again. How would they know?"

Elijah's feet dropped to the floor with a thud. "The only way they could go back in time with you is to possess you, since they have no physical body here. I suspect they're guessing at this point. You haven't time walked that I know of, or have you?"

"I haven't, but I have to send them back, Elijah, before they realize I can. And I have to close the portal from this side."

"For fuck's sake, Celine. Absolutely not. You're not ready."

"You can't stop me."

She gulped when he rose from his chair and leaned over with both hands braced on the wood. Black eyes narrowed to thin slits and lit with flames. "Try me."

Her chin lifted. "Are you threatening me?"

"No. I'm promising to protect you. I'll bind your soul so fucking tight you won't be able to breathe."

There it was again...the emotion in his eyes. This was his way of showing he cared. The hint of a smile lifted the corner of her lips. "Thank you, Elijah."

His lips firmed into a tight line.

"I'm sorry I attacked you earlier."

He growled. "Stop it. I liked it. A lot."

"I think the beast has a heart after all," she teased with a wink.

"Fuck you, Celine," he grumbled, storming from the room. "I like you better when you're a smartass."

And she chuckled when the door slammed.

*****

There were very few people who crawled under his skin, but Celine did from the moment he saw her. He stomped to his room in the basement and removed his clothes with a thought. A hot shower and a nap sounded like the best way to relieve the stress of the day. Having her here was a nightmare, but he couldn't stand the idea of her anywhere else.

He stepped under the hot spray and moaned when water sluiced over his flesh. If ever a woman tempted him, it was Celine. She was hot in the club, but the necromancer identity seduced him from the inside out. It was time to admit defeat.

One hand cupped his balls and slid the length of his dick. He'd been hard and miserable from that night when her gift caressed his, coaxing it from his soul with black magic and desire. He wanted to lick every inch to show his full appreciation and fuck her senseless to claim her, maybe beat her ass. Holding their bond a hairbreadth from the total union was agonizing pain, firing from every nerve like a bad acid trip.

He needed her. That frustrated him to no end and caused him to say things he didn't mean. And she had to be nice. The sickening sweet shit seeped out of her and clung to his skin.

Elijah hung his head, water pouring from his hair, stroking himself, and imagining her laid out before him like a fucking buffet. He would feast until she squirmed on his tongue, drenching his face in liquid fire and necromancer magic.

Engorged and on fire, his muscles tensed as cum shot from the slit, swirling into the drain when it should be inside her teasing little pussy. The tightness eased, but roared back to life as soon as he thought of her again. His eyes rolled to the ceiling in frustration.

He finished his shower, dried off and dropped on his bed, but his head lifted when he noticed the pale pink color of his sheets, the fluffed pillows, and flowered comforter. A chuckle rumbled from his chest, and he rolled onto his back, staring at the flowered, ruffled curtains surrounding his bed. How'd she do that without him knowing?

He grabbed a pillow and tucked it under his head, drifting in and out of sleep for thirty minutes, when he bolted upright. His gaze lifted to the ceiling, and his head tilted. Something dark whispered in the room, and he jumped from the bed. What was that? He turned in a circle, searching for the source.

"Celine," he growled, running from the room.

*****

She fixated on the book once Elijah left the study. It called to her with the promise of knowledge. She gnawed on her thumbnail and rearranged his pens and pencils.

"Time walker," it tempted in a sweet voice like her mothers. Twice she ignored it, but the third time she scooped it off the desk and sat on the sofa in front of the fireplace.

Fingers trailed over the familiar leather, scraping the worn edges. Captivated, she opened it, skimming through the pages. The pads of her fingers traced her mother's handwriting, trying to decipher the scribbles and diagrams. She fanned the pages with one hand, the palm of the other hand hovering above them, allowing the book to show her where it wanted her to go.

The pages suspended in midair and opened for her. Elijah's name was there, linked to hers with a line between them in blue ink. Celine's eyes widened, reading the words out loud.

98

In the future, I found him. Elijah Drake, King of the Unseelie. The harnesser for my daughter.

Her mother knew.

Celine continued to read, scanning through the pages until they became something she didn't understand. The script was foreign, the marks of the pencil jagged as if the writer pressed too hard. Shaded symbols lined the edge of the pages, the pencil lead blurred or smudged.

Incantations covered the next few pages. Spells of strength, wisdom, and protection written for the family. It was clear her mother was still in her right mind when she wrote them. She flipped to the last few entries and frowned at the difference in the handwriting and the language used.

Summon Daemonium, in bold script, covered the pages.

Her mouth moved, sounding the word out. She knew what it meant, and almost had it when Elijah jerked the book from her hands.

"No, Celine." He tossed it in the fireplace, and flames engulfed it.

She knew he wouldn't do it without good reason, and the glare radiating from his eyes reinforced the notion.

"It's a word used for legions in hell. Don't ever speak it, Celine. Don't summon them. Ever."

*****

He knew better than to leave the book with Celine. It was spelled, true, but also cursed. He saw the evidence himself. "I'm sorry. I know it was important to you."

"I don't understand, Elijah. Tell me."

"They tormented your mother in the end. I should've destroyed the book."

"But we're together now."

"We haven't bonded completely. I won't take a chance with your life, and neither should you. Didn't you learn your fucking lesson at home?"

One eyebrow arched over her flaming eyes, and his dick twitched. Damn, that was hot.

"I know what to look for now," rushed out of her mouth.

"No, you don't. You proved that last time. And it doesn't matter because I haven't fully harnessed you yet. We're not bonded."

"You did rather well in the yard until Laura showed up. How can I depend on you when you flinch if she speaks your name?"

Celine spat the words, and he almost grinned.

"Are you jealous?"

She jerked upright. "Jealous of a ghost or demon? No. I'm disappointed I've been attached to a mate with a chip on his shoulder and a hangup on his ex-girlfriend."

"I don't have a problem. You do though."

"I don't," she quickly stammered.

He rose from the fireplace once he was sure the book burned. She jumped from the couch and strolled to his desk. He followed, but she darted to the opposite end. "Why are you afraid of me?"

"I'm not."

He slid one finger over the top of his desk. "Then why are you running from me?"

"I don't know. You just have this weird look."

"Have you had sex before, Celine?"

Her chin lifted. "Not that it's any of your concern, but yes."

She squeaked when her clothes instantly disappeared and attempted to cover herself.

His eyes slithered over exposed, creamy flesh, and his mouth watered. "I'm going to lick and fuck every inch of you. We will bond. No more risks."

She backed toward the corner when he jumped over the desk. "Before anything else happens, I'm going to make sure we're bound so tightly together, nothing can ever touch your soul except me. Before you do something stupid, I'm going to give you a reason to reconsider."

"You said you didn't want me. I heard you."

With one hand, he knocked everything off his desk, then yanked her by the waist into his arms. "I lied. You should know, I lie a lot."

She opened her mouth to argue, and he captured it, sweeping his tongue inside. Small hands pressed against his shoulders, but in ten seconds, something odd happened. Her tongue met his, swirling with heat, and her hands threaded into his hair.

His clothing disappeared, and her nipples grazed his chest, bringing a growl. His hands trailed down her spine to grip her bare ass and massage the globes.

Celine gasped when he lifted her from the floor and laid her on his desk, but she didn't object. Both hands skated over the front of her body, teasing, twisting, and pinching her nipples before tracing the dip of her waist and flare of her hips.

The sweet aroma of her arousal filled his nostrils, and he inhaled deeply. "I wonder if you're wet for me?"

With two fingers, he caressed her pink folds and groaned when he found her slick with desire. "Good girl," he hissed and sat in his chair.

"Soak my face, Celine."

He didn't give her time to think, grasped her thighs, and slid her pussy to his mouth. She wanted words of adoration, but he wasn't a man to give them. Instead, he would show her with his tongue and fingers.

A sigh escaped when he teased her opening and curled his tongue against her walls. She squirmed, but he only tongue fucked her faster until she dripped with cum for him and moaned with pleasure.

"Fucking delicious," he mouthed against her.

Her thighs spread wider, and he slid two fingers deep into her channel. With her pussy full, he paid homage to her clit, sucking until she arched off the desk in reckless abandon. Her hands gripped the sides as he claimed and punished her body without mercy.

He wasn't a gentle lover and never had been.

With his tongue, he traced her folds until he reached her nub and sucked it into his mouth. His dick throbbed, pre-cum leaking from the slit, wanting to be buried in her tight channel, but he was intent on bringing her pleasure first.

Perfect tits filled his vision, her pink nipples stiff and begging to be sucked. His free hand splayed over her abdomen, sliding higher until he could flick those little buds with his fingers, pinch, and caress.

She cried out, her legs clamping the side of his shoulders. Juices soaked his fingers and hand. Her little pussy fucked his face, drenching his mouth. He wanted her dripping cum and begging for relief before he fucked her. She moaned when he slapped his palm against her folds. The rough play caused his dick to thicken and twitch.

"Fucking come for me, Celine. I want it all."

And she did on a hoarse cry, covering his mouth in delicious cream. Her body tremored from the orgasm as she rocked into his fingers, her pelvis jerking to be fuller, fucking his face until he wrung the last drop from her tight pussy.

She rose from the desk as he rose from his chair and positioned the head of his dick against her slick folds. Three times he slid his cock up and down, teasing her opening before backing away.

Her hips rotated with each movement, coating him in wet heat. Engorged and hard as a stone, he ran his hand along his shaft, teasing her, teasing himself until his teeth clenched together.

Legs dangled on either side of his hips, soft thighs rubbing against him. Her lips touched his chest, and she sucked a nipple into her mouth, circling it with her tongue. His head fell back to gaze at the ceiling, her mouth moving between his nipples. A small hand joined his, stroking his dick and teasing his balls. Nails scraped the underside softly, featherlight touches that had him moaning with desire. When she bit his nipple, his entire body tightened. She took control of his dick, rubbing the head through her folds, fucking the one inch he allowed her to have.

Both hands slid over her shoulders and down her back. She moved closer, her greedy pussy clenching and needing filled. Her nipples grazed his stomach. One hand cupped his ass and squeezed, coaxing him closer. Nails dug into his flesh when her mouth latched onto his skin, and she began to bite and suck.

Was she fucking marking him? He hoped so.

One hand fisted her hair at the nape, and he jerked her head back when he couldn't take anymore, gripping the strands roughly. She bit her lip at the sting but didn't complain. Her thighs spread wider, and her pelvis slid forward, claiming another inch of his dick. She liked this.

"You want fucked hard? Beg for my dick, baby. I need to hear you say it."

Her lips parted, and her tongue flicked her lips. Heels dug into the backs of his thighs. She rolled her pelvis, her perfect pussy sucking at his dick. Her eyes narrowed, and black magic swirled in the air. His head tilted as flames engulfed her eyes. She hissed when he refused to allow her more of his dick. "Against the wall, Elijah."

He lifted her and slammed her back into the wall behind his desk. Celine was wild and on fire for him, fucking perfect in every way.

"Is this what you want?" he asked, trapping her hands above her head, and pressing fully against her.

Flame filled eyes locked with his, but slowly lowered to his mouth. "Yes."

Her back arched, nipples sliding against his chest. Eyes closed, breasts lifted, hair a tangled mess about her shoulders, he paused just to gaze at the one created for him. Her tongue slicked across her full bottom lip, and his gaze narrowed. The pulse point at the base of her throat throbbed, but he didn't have the urge to feed anymore.

Her thighs hugged his waist, and her small feet locked at the base of his spine. Warmth emanated from her core, and for the first time in years, his body was hot.

In that instance, he realized he needed more. The tethers to his soul expanded in white ropes and extended from his body to caress her skin, sliding between her legs to tease her pussy. One rope circled a nipple, tightening on the bud. Celine sighed into his mouth, and he claimed her lips with bruising force.

She was so beautiful, so sexy, and she belonged to him.

He allowed her body to slide down the wall until the head of his dick penetrated her, stopping with a tortuous groan. How easy it would be to claim her, but he wanted something else, something he'd never had. His head fell against her bare shoulder, and he released her hands. He smacked the wall beside her face. "Give me more, Celine. Tell me what you feel."

*****

The first time she laid eyes on him in the club, she knew.

The first time he touched her, confirmed it.

His soul called to hers even as he backed away. She watched him leave, the powerful width of his shoulders moving through the people. The loss made her want to weep once he disappeared. She may not have known what the soul bond was, what harnesser or tethered meant, but she recognized the magic, the matching tourmaline, and even called his magic to her.

His touch was electrifying and powerful, and her soul reached for his compassion and protection, but he wanted her secrets. It was too much.

The tip of his dick slid inside her, stretching her, tempting her to confess everything. He would destroy her. The ropes of his soul caressed her body in sensual strokes, stoking the flames hotter. He asked her to voice the innermost emotion she didn't want to reveal yet. They were connected, so he had to know.

It seemed like a weakness to voice the truth, a weapon he would use to break her.

"Look at me, Celine. See your mate."

She turned away at first, refusing the command, but slowly pivoted her gaze. Hot tears leaked from her eyes and burned over her cheeks. So beautiful. So desperate. This man thought he loved once, but there was a loneliness in his black eyes only she could see. He hurt as much as she did, the soul bond weeping between them.

"I knew the moment I saw you," she whispered, hoping to appease him so he'd end this torture.

His hand smacked the wall above her. "That's not enough. What are you fucking afraid of?"

He demanded the answer she didn't want to give.

"That you're only with me because you were forced," she choked out, but she knew better, and he knew the truth.

His hand smacked the wall again as his dick slid inside her a little more. "That's bullshit. Does it feel like I don't want to be with you? Give it all to me, Celine."

He sighed against her shoulder, his lips kissing tenderly. "I need to hear it," he groaned. "Even if it's a lie."

Her gaze lifted from his blond head to the ceiling as more tears fell. The agony in his voice pierced her heart with talons, burrowing deep and twisting her soul. Bared completely naked physically and emotionally, she choked back a sob.

"I'm afraid you can't love me," she cried out.

"Tell me, Celine. Say what's in your heart. Tell me what you feel when you see me!" he commanded one more time.

She inhaled a deep breath for courage, fighting the words, but losing the battle. Love shouldn't be war, but he stalked her on the battlefield with weapons of desire and desperation.

Her eyes closed when he lifted his head. Warm lips pressed to the corners of hers, and his tongue slid across the seam of her mouth. Tender seduction became his weapon, and she craved more, always wanted more, desperate for this man's affection. His dick slid deeper, her walls contracting on his length, needing all of him the same way he begged for her.

"I love you," she whispered so low, she didn't think she'd actually given the words a voice.

"You love a monster," he growled, but the ropes of his soul pierced her skin, burrowing, digging, tunneling until they penetrated hers. He allowed her body to fully sheath him, and she sighed with the rightness. For the first time in her life, she belonged. And it didn't matter if she belonged to a monster.

Her hands threaded into his hair, and his face dropped to her chest. She could only hold on when his mouth surrounded one nipple, rolling the sensitive bud between his teeth. Her back arched from the wall even as his hands released hers to slide along her sides and grip her ass with bruising force. He spread her cheeks, plunging deeper into her body.

Her spine scraped the wall with each tight thrust, and his teeth nipped at her flesh, sucking certain spots until she was sure he'd marked her. Every part of her was full and on fire, close to exploding. His mouth moved to the space where her shoulder and neck met, teeth scraping. She held her breath when he bit her hard enough to break the skin. The blood was what he knew, but the bond was something he couldn't fight.

"I love you," she spoke a little stronger, and his ropes secured her soul like protective bands. An impenetrable shield locked in place.

His movements ceased to be jerky and fueled by anger but became gentle with caresses that sent her blood humming in her veins. He sucked at her neck, and she held him to her. His mouth moved upward and nipped her earlobe, eliciting a shiver.

"I need you, Celine," he whispered in her ear, and she melted.

He never returned a deeper sentiment, but it didn't matter because she heard the desperation and the truth in his voice.

No longer did he squeeze but massaged. Long swipes of his tongue trailed down her neck and across her shoulder. His lips tasted her flesh like she was fine wine, and his hips rolled into her instead of tightly thrusting. Her core spasmed close to the edge, and he groaned.

Her hands slid over his shoulders before returning to his perfect face. With her fingers, she lifted his chin to gaze at his features. Black eyes smoldered with glowing embers, threatening to burn her to ashes. Black wings expanded from his back to hover on either side of his body.

"Don't be afraid," he whispered huskily.

"I'm not afraid, Elijah."

Dark magic linked with the strands securing her to him. Genuine passion, not lust, exploded, and she tremored with sensual need. Tingles expanded from her core, and her pussy contracted, the spasms rippling over his dick. His hands trapped hers, holding her in place, and his tongue threaded into her mouth, stroking and claiming. The necromancer's power unleashed and exploded over them both, her orgasm shaking the stone foundation of the house.

At the same moment, Elijah held completely still, and his seed spurted in hot ropes to bathe her inner walls and thighs. His tongue swirled in her mouth. There was no beginning and no end to them.

This was what she wanted and didn't have the courage to ask for.

He held her against the wall, kissing and licking every spot he'd nipped. Tremors wracked her body, slowly subsiding in the aftermath. Her fingers slid through his hair, fanning it to either side of his shoulders. He inhaled her skin, running his nose up her neck.

Black eyes locked with hers. "I'm exhausted. I haven't slept in years. Will you sleep beside me, Celine?" he murmured against her lips.

She nodded because that was all she could do, and he carried her to a bedroom deep within the lower level of his home. She didn't ask when he laid her on a bed, closing the drapes surrounding it. This was his sanctuary when he was a vampire. *Old habits die hard*, she mused to herself as he slid into the bed behind her. She reached for the flowered curtains and smiled when thick arms secured her waist. A sigh escaped as he nuzzled the back of her hair.

"Angel?" She had to know.

"Descendent from the Nephilim."

"The giants? That's why you're so tall? And the wings?"

"I'm a genetic anomaly. All Unseelie are. Not angel, not demon, somewhere in between."

Celine stroked his arm with her fingertips. "Perfect is what you are."

"You shouldn't tell lies," he growled against her back, but his lips lifted in a small smile against her skin. "I'm the only one permitted to lie. Go to sleep, Celine."

How humbling to realize this man loved when she assumed he couldn't. How remarkable to know he needed to hear the words from her, and no one else. And she would love him hard.

Chapter 6

Bed. Warm. Soft. Smelled like Celine.

Elijah pulled the blankets over his head, enjoying this little thing he'd missed. The sleep of the dead wasn't anything compared to this. He didn't want to open his eyes until he heard Ara laugh, followed by Jax and Celine. Their voices drifted through the floor, and he ran one hand over his face in annoyance. "What the hell are they doing here?"

With a groan, he rolled onto his stomach, only to inhale Celine's delicate scent on his pink sheets. A snarl escaped from the corner of his lip while he replayed everything that happened between them.

What the fuck was wrong with him? He didn't love, but he sure as hell almost professed it. He wanted things he never thought to have with her. And she fucked like a champ, glowed under his dominance, and rode the edge of pain and pleasure with him.

This mate business was no joke, and Celine stripped his soul with her confession.

There were no windows at this lower level, and darkness surrounded him. It was time for a change, starting with moving the bedroom upstairs and ditching the Dracula aesthetic.

More laughter came from above, and his eyes lifted to the ceiling. Ara would be a gloating pig today, and Jax had taken an unappreciated interest in his mate. Fucking dragons. Why didn't they stay on their mountain where they belonged?

A growl rumbled from his stomach when the scent of coffee drifted to him along with breakfast foods. He hadn't eaten actual food in years, and it smelled damn good.

After yanking on a pair of sweats, but no shirt, he stumbled upstairs and into the kitchen. He leaned against the doorframe and watched the three chatting like they were long lost best friends. Celine held a mug to her full lips, and he imagined licking the coffee from her mouth. Ara glanced between the pair while Jax talked some nonsense about time walking.

"She's not time walking with you," he grumbled.

Everyone turned their attention to him, but his gaze settled on Celine.

"How can I learn how if I don't try?"

Her question was innocent enough, but he didn't like it. Time walking would put her in a vulnerable situation. "It's not safe yet."

Her eyebrows lifted. "It will never be safe, and I can't sit here knowing I let them out."

"Who?" Ara asked.

"Demons," Celine stated, without taking her attention from him.

"No."

"What can they do after last night?" A blush spread across her cheeks, but she didn't lower her eyes.

"They can attack your mind and make your life a living hell."

"What if I could go back and change everything I did? There was something off with my client, anyway. That's when it started. She lied about her reasons."

"Tampering with the timeline is dangerous for everyone," Jax added.

"How so?" Celine asked.

Elijah moved toward the coffeepot and grabbed a mug. "You could make it fucking worse, for one."

"Aren't you all gloom and doom this morning," Ara snorted.

"I just speak the truth. It doesn't matter if the client lied. What matters is what they hoped to gain and preventing it."

"By finding the doorway into this realm," Celine supplied.

"And there's the riddle. Where is this supposed doorway to hell?" Elijah grumbled, pouring himself a cup of coffee.

"Tristan might know," Ara suggested.

"I don't know, but my father did, I think." Tristan walked into the house like he owned it, with Nena on his arm.

Elijah swore at his uninvited guests. "Why is everyone here so early on the first morning after I actually slept in years? Give me one good fucking reason."

"Demon," Celine shrieked, moving toward him.

"Oh, for fuck's sake, Tristan. She's necromancer."

Tristan tossed one hand in the air. "What do you want me to do? It's not like I can stuff him in a jar."

Nena smiled sweetly. "Not demon, but the Spirit of the Fae. Tristan carries the burden since he's Fae King."

"Hey everyone. Sorry we're late to the party," Stevie laughed, handing Matthew to Tristan.

"Baby stuff," Dagen grumbled as an excuse.

"You let him hold your baby with that thing beside him?" Celine asked incredulously.

"What thing?" Stevie answered. "Tristan is Matthew's favorite person."

"That black shadow," Celine said, pointing at Tristan.

Stevie glanced at Tristan and Nena. "She can see it?"

"Necromancer," Tristan replied.

Elijah sat his coffee a little too hard on the counter. "Can I just have a cup of fucking coffee before it gets any weirder?" And stomped to his study, leaving Celine to stare, and everyone else to explain.

"Someone is cranky in the morning," Ara chuckled.

"I can hear you, dragon!" Elijah shouted, before slamming his door so hard the entire house rattled.

*****

"I don't know how to manage him sometimes," Celine whispered, hoping no one heard, but desperately needing advice.

"Things have a way of working out," Stevie commented, moving a little closer.

"He's so gruff."

"He's always been like that," Ara said, nodding toward the study. "But he has a heart of gold and would do anything for anybody. Tristan, Elijah, and I used to play together as kids."

Celine smiled. "I can't imagine him as a child."

Ara chuckled. "Always in trouble, always grumbling about something, but that is Elijah's way. He's protective of you, though, Celine. I saw it before he entered the room."

"And I saw it yesterday," Jax snorted.

Celine glanced toward the closed door as an idea struck. "That shadow thing you carry around, Tristan? It would pass as a demon easily."

"And?" Tristan asked.

"You said your father knew where the doorway was, so I'm assuming you don't. Could your spirit or shadow or whatever it is fool a demon?"

"Possibly, but I'd have to be close. Too close for comfort. My father messed with that stuff, and it destroyed him after my mother passed."

117

"If I time walked us..."

"No," Stevie answered for him. "It's too dangerous. Listen to me, Celine. There are no answers in the past or with a demon. Your future is here."

Jax shifted in his seat. "She's right. Any or all of you could become lost in the time shift, with demons hounding your every step. They want you on their plane. It's manipulation."

"What about the spirit? I've entered the Domain of Souls a hundred times."

Jax shook his head. "Which is something you shouldn't have done. You know this, Celine. The longer you're out of your body, the harder it is to come back. Time is limited on that plane. It's not an option."

"Even when I've been harnessed?"

Jax's gaze met hers. "Elijah is the only one who could go with you and would be forced to watch you slip slowly into their world. It's a drug, Celine. You can't trust spirits, especially demons."

"The Druids covered us in some type of shield."

"It's a protective barrier for this side only. You're panicking, Celine, grasping at straws," Jax scolded, crossing his arms.

Celine frowned and rolled her eyes to the ceiling. "I have to fix this. I need to go back to the beginning to make it right. You guys don't understand."

"I understand," Nena interjected. "I understand more than anything wanting to change the past, but it's dangerous, Celine. Things happen for a reason. Demons won't give you answers. They'll give you lies and have you running in circles until you're so dizzy you can't find your way out."

The door to Elijah's study crashed open and banged against the wall. Fire lit his eyes as he stomped toward her like a savage beast, stopping directly before her. "If we go back in time, then we go all the way, Celine. It seems like that's the only thing that will make you happy."

"I just want to fix it."

"No. You want to fucking meddle, so let's meddle. We'll fuck up everything so bad that no one will have a chance."

"That's not fair, Elijah."

"Not fair?" he asked. "We should find the fucking portal in the Fae realm instead of chase ghosts and demons, but you can't stop because you're addicted to it."

"I'm not," she shouted.

"You're just like Laura. Addicted to those things instead of living a real life."

Celine took a step back. Was that true? Had she become hooked on seeking answers from the dead? She'd done it for so long, she'd spent more time with spirits than real people. Her gaze lifted to Elijah, and the fierce emotion in his black eyes. He'd lost one woman to that life, and she'd witnessed what it did to her mother. Everyone here warned her. Her mother warned her repeatedly and even stopped her training. Elijah was right. "If I am, I don't want to be."

The tenseness left his shoulders, and he held out one hand. "Then choose me, Celine. Choose us. Choose to live in the present."

It was a pivotal moment in their rocky relationship and with everyone watching. "You didn't want me two days ago."

His face tilted. "How can you still think that after what happened between us? I may not have said it, but you felt it."

Her heart thudded hard in her chest, and her eyes lowered to his hand. She remembered how desperately he asked for her love, how tender his touch turned when she gave it freely, and the strength and protection she experienced in his arms. It was the greatest moment of her life, realizing he needed her as much as she needed him.

Her palm slid against his, their fingers locked, and he yanked her against his chest. This was where she belonged...with this living, warm soul.

"Thank you, Elijah," she whispered against his chest. "I lost my way."

One hand slid down the back of her hair.

"Well, I never thought I'd see the day," Ara snorted.

"Shut up, Ara," Elijah barked over her head.

"Looks like Elijah taught the lesson Wilma asked me to teach." Jax laughed.

"Fucking old crone," Elijah growled.

Matthew chose that moment to chuckle out loud, staring at Elijah.

"What are you laughing at, baby?" Elijah grumbled.

But Matthew chuckled again.

"Looks like you've lost your edge, vampire," Dagen teased.

Celine lifted her face in time to see Elijah wink. Her tummy fluttered even as he snarled, "Damn werewolves. You don't even know me, so why are you in my house?"

Stevie arched one eyebrow. "I think you know us pretty well by now."

"Exhibitionism is hot," Elijah taunted. "You should've chosen your spot better."

Dagen grunted when Stevie smacked his chest. "You had to run naked in the moonlight, didn't you?"

A chuckle rumbled from Dagen. "That's normal for Lycan."

Elijah snorted. "You think you're normal?"

When Matthew laughed so hard, Tristan had to tighten his hold, everyone laughed.

*****

"Now what?" Celine asked.

"We find the entrance, and we seal it."

"The answers might be in the library," Tristan suggested.

"There's a library?" Elijah questioned. "Sounds boring."

"Dusty and full of old scripts. It holds all records for all people and locations within the Fae Kingdom," Tristan answered.

Elijah leaned against the counter with Celine positioned between his legs. "Then that's where we start."

"That won't be necessary."

All faces turned to Bianca entering the kitchen. "I know where it is. The knowledge transferred to me after Danu's death. It's in an isolated and dangerous part of Fae."

Jax rose from his chair. The tension in the room increased ten notches as the pair made eye contact, but it quickly vanished.

Elijah glanced between the pair and at everyone else in the room. These were his friends, some from childhood, and he wouldn't put their lives in danger. "Celine and I will go. Alone."

Bianca moved to the center of the room. "Celine, Stevie, and Nena...do you have your stones?"

The women glanced at each other.

"I have the uncut diamond," Celine commented.

"The peridot is in my ring," Nena answered.

"And I have the moonstone." Stevie lifted the necklace from her chest for Bianca, her mother, and Jax, her father, to see.

Bianca faced Tristan. "The stone my mother returned to you. Not Nena's wedding ring."

Tristan's eyes widened. "I wondered why she returned it."

"Danu always had a reason." Bianca addressed the group again. "The fourth queen hasn't come into power yet. Without her stone, you can't fully seal the entrance to hell, but you can make it difficult."

Bianca turned toward Celine. "It's unwise to communicate with the dead, but you'll need to send the ones you brought into the human world back to where they came from. It can only be done once the doorway is closed and from within the Domain of Souls, Celine. Trust your harnesser."

"I'll go with them," Jax stated, rising from his seat.

Bianca turned to him. "No. You're needed at the Dragon Council."

"What could the Dragon Council possibly want with me?" Jax asked, perplexed.

Bianca faced Ara. "Aramand's mate has fallen, but your mate lives. Do you understand?"

"That's not possible," Ara hissed, rising from her seat at the table. "Tobias passed in the war. His family died in the battle with Tristan's father."

"He lives, Ara. And he's in trouble," Bianca said gently.

Elijah cleared his throat. "Excuse me? What does that mean for Ara and Aramand?"

Bianca smiled at Ara. "It means Ara will become the fourth queen."

"Oh shit," Elijah laughed. "A hot-headed fire dragon on the throne."

"She deserves this for what she did for the kingdom," Tristan said, laying one hand on Ara's shoulder.

"I don't want to be queen. I never planned for this. It was always Aramand," Ara spoke to everyone. "What will my brother do? Always be alone?"

"He'll find love again," Bianca barely whispered, glancing at Jax. "Death is imminent, but love is not."

Jax's lips twitched, and a tiny smile lifted the corners of his mouth.

Bianca took Matthew from Tristan. "Now that everyone has their tasks, you and I get to spend time together, grandson." She waved one hand, and a portal opened in the kitchen. "Safe travels to the six."

A second portal opened on the opposite side of the kitchen, and Bianca faced Ara and Jax. "Safe journey, you two. And Ara, not all is what it seems. Remember to listen to the heart, not the fire."

Bianca cooed at Matthew as their forms shimmered and dissipated, leaving the rest of the party gaping at each other.

"Well, that was awkward," Elijah grumbled.

"Did she just disappear? With your baby?" Celine asked.

"She's Goddess," Stevie answered. "And my mother."

"Interfering mother," Dagen growled.

*****

124

Celine's spine straightened when everyone froze, and her mouth gaped as Bianca and Matthew reappeared. Light surrounded them both, eyes swirling with gold. She glanced at everyone in the room, but they weren't moving anymore. Her eyes returned to Bianca.

"Is this a vision or something?"

Bianca nodded at Ara. "I wanted to speak to you privately. Ara's mate needs you."

"Me?" Celine asked, perplexed. "I don't know him. I don't know anyone that well."

"You know what happened to your mother?"

"Demons tormented her. Don't worry. I listened to Elijah and everyone else. I don't need another lecture."

"No lecture, Celine. You're young, but you're also wise and gifted. There are people in this world who assume madness is a physical ailment, but you know different."

"Correct."

"There will come a time when you have to choose between saving Ara's mate, and altering your timeline, but listen closely to me when I say choose wisely. You wouldn't have met Elijah if events hadn't happened the way they did, and the portal into the Fae realm can't be closed without Ara's stone. This world and the human realm will cease to exist if you choose incorrectly. Your mother knew this. She time walked to find your harnesser."

"You're saying the attack on Ara's mate, and I was planned?"

Bianca bounced Matthew in arms. "With two queens in power…"

"They plotted against the two remaining queens," Celine finished the sentence. "I'm the third, but Ara can't ascend as the fourth queen without her mate."

"And the dragons are susceptible to what they label madness," Bianca explained.

"Which would be easy to assume was of the mind, not demonic."

"Exactly," Bianca confirmed. "Your mother wasn't insane. She was tormented. The effects were devastating for her, but know that she ensured you wouldn't be alone."

"And this task we're getting ready to embark on?"

Bianca winked. "Everything happens for a reason."

"That's cryptic."

"I can't interfere anymore, Celine. I'm here to guide, not choose. And on that note, Elijah will do anything to protect you, even with lies. Remember that when you face indecision or doubt."

"What do you mean?"

"Some people prove how they feel with action instead of words. Trust the soul bond."

Celine frowned when Bianca disappeared for good.

Chapter 7

Elijah assumed the lead with Celine close behind, and together they entered a paradise-like landscape. The others followed.

Magnificent flower blooms in red and orange contrasted with dark green foliage. Waterfalls fell onto great bodies of water, but steam or a gaseous type of substance hovered over them. There were no fish or animals. And the ground was sand with jagged stones one could easily trip on. It was a beautiful but deadly wasteland.

"Don't touch anything," Tristan warned, exiting the portal.

"Why?" Dagen asked.

"Poisonous. Everything you see is deadly. My father spoke of this place. He called it The Opposite," Tristan explained.

Stevie lifted her gaze to the sky and the twin purple moons. "It's still part of Fae lands, though. Right?"

Elijah pulled Celine to his side, not wanting her out of his sight. "The outermost faction of the Fae realm. My parents spoke of it since we were Unseelie. The darkest of the dark live here, and the Fae with a wish to die come here. They warned me to never enter."

Nena turned in a circle. "It's so beautiful."

"Evil can be beautiful too," Elijah commented. "Remember, Lucifer was the most beautiful angel before he fell."

"The doorway could be anywhere," Celine said, glancing everywhere.

Stevie pointed toward a cliff face. "It's there. I feel it." Her head tilted. "It's beckoning us to come. Do you hear it?"

"That's demon-speak," Celine hissed. "Ignore it."

Elijah listened closely to the chanting, but motioned to Dagen and Tristan when their mates moved forward. "Get them out of here."

Dagen grabbed Stevie's hand, preventing her from going any farther. "We're not leaving you to face this alone," he growled, and yanked Stevie into his arms.

Elijah shook his head. "Give me the stones."

Tristan grabbed Nena from behind. "No."

"Your mates are in danger. Nena is pregnant. Get them out of here now. They want the queens," Elijah reminded.

"You understand that language?" Tristan asked.

"I understand, and it's nothing you want to know. Now leave before I force you out."

Dagen shook his head. "Come with us. You and Celine. We'll find another way."

Celine lifted her eyes to him. "We can't. I'm afraid more than anyone, but you know it's true."

Elijah slid one down her back, but his lips firmed. "We're a harnessed pair. She is a necromancer, and I'm her harnesser. We can't leave."

Tristan opened a portal. "What can we do?"

"Find Jax and Bianca. Tell them they are already here. They'll know what it means. Celine and I'll place the stones, but we need Ara's."

Tristan tossed the Peridot of Kings at his feet, and Dagen lifted the moonstone necklace from Stevie's neck. Elijah scooped them from the ground and placed them in his pocket next to Celine's uncut diamond.

Elijah swore when Nena's eyes swirled with purple magic. Tristan struggled to hold her, and Dagen was experiencing the same problem with Stevie. "I'm sorry," he mouthed to Tristan, allowing his soul to expand. White ropes rose in the air, whipped with an audible snap, and forcefully shoved them through the portal.

With a growl, Dagen lifted Stevie in his arms and ran inside the light.

"It seems I've lied again," Elijah murmured, kissing Celine's forehead.

Her brow wrinkled in confusion. "Elijah? What do you mean?"

"We have to time walk and enter the Domain of Souls."

Celine faced the cliff. "You said I shouldn't."

"You won't be alone this time."

"I haven't time walked."

Elijah frowned at his mate's upturned face. She doubted herself. "When the time comes, let your magic flow. Speak it, and I'll follow. I'll always follow you."

"What if we get separated or worse? What if I can't find my way back? What if..."

Elijah held up one hand. "I've harnessed you, Celine. I need you to wage war like you did at your house. Don't be a fucking pussy."

At once, her countenance changed, and he saw the spark in her eyes.

"There you are. Ready?"

Celine inhaled a deep breath. "Ready. I don't know what I'm looking for, though."

"A place the stones will fit. You'll know it when you see it."

******

The closer they moved toward the cliff, the louder the chanting became. Celine gripped Elijah's hand.

"Never show fear, Celine."

She knew he was right, needed his reassurance, but a hundred doubts churned in her mind. "What are those markings?"

"Latin demonic symbols."

"That's inviting," she snorted.

"Makes you feel welcome, right?"

Celine stopped when the chanting turned to screams. "They know we're here."

"They knew as soon as we stepped through the portal."

"Is that a cave?" Celine asked, pointing toward a dome-shaped entrance. "Why aren't they coming out?"

"Because I'm going in. Alone."

Celine jerked when a portal suddenly opened, and nine men stepped through to circle them. "What's going on?"

Elijah grabbed her hand and placed the stones in her palm. "Seal the entrance once Ara ascends as queen."

Her eyes dropped to the stones. "What are you doing, Elijah?"

"Making it right."

"How? I don't understand."

"Laura has agreed to leave you and the Fae realm alone if I willingly go with her."

"She lies, Elijah. She's a demon. That's what they do."

His gaze lowered to the ground. "I still love her."

Celine flinched as if she'd been struck. "We're harnessed, Elijah. You can't possibly mean that after what you told me. After what happened between us?"

"My men are going to harness you to protect you, just in case."

"No. Look at me, Elijah. Look me in the eye and tell me you don't love me." Anger boiled in her gut, and her magic flared wildly. This couldn't be happening.

His face lifted, and the power of the Unseelie King extended from his body.

"You're a liar, Elijah. How many times have you said it yourself?"

The ropes securing her soul loosened, circled her body, then expanded outward, but one remained. Her face tilted. "If you don't love me, then let go completely," she dared, moving one step closer to him.

He shook his head as ropes from the souls of his men circled her waist and penetrated her flesh.

"No, Elijah. I'd rather be alone. They can't harness my heart because it's yours."

The ropes pierced her, securing her soul with those of strangers just as Laura materialized beside Elijah.

"Hello queen without a king," she sneered.

But Celine refused to remove her focus from Elijah. His black eyes were fathomless, but she saw the authentic emotion there. And it hadn't wavered. He loved her no matter what he said. This was his way of protecting her.

Bianca's words surfaced in her mind. Even Elijah described himself as a liar.

Ropes tightened around her soul, suffocating and unfamiliar.

No one else should harness her except Elijah. No one else could fully harness her.

"Liar," she whispered.

"You know me better than anyone, Celine. Look in my soul for the truth."

Her gaze didn't leave his, even when her mother's voice spoke into her mind, clear and true.

Touch his hand where the demon can't see, think of where you want to go, and repeat after me.

I manipulate time
Bend it to my will

Where I go
No demon will
Weaving the threads
Is my gift
Time splits apart
As I enter the rift

Celine recited the words with one finger grazing Elijah's hand. He never moved or acknowledged the connection. And Laura didn't notice.

A smirk lifted the corners of his mouth, and Celine understood. Matter bent before her eyes, the world retracted, blinding light flashed, and the strands of time revealed themselves to her.

Laura screeched, her spirited body disappearing in a smoky haze.

Celine's power expanded rapidly. The world fell away, and they entered a tunnel of light. Elijah's men trailed behind them, still attached to her soul by their ropes.

"Where are we going, time walker?" Elijah asked.

"The beginning. And if you lie to me again, I'll leave you there."

Elijah chuckled, reaching for her when they landed on the pavement with a thud. His men grumbled and cursed out loud.

"Sorry. Rough landing," Celine laughed.

But Elijah rolled on top of her. "You didn't really believe that bullshit, did you?"

Her fingers traced the angle of his jaw. "Oh, you reeked of lies."

"It was the only way. She found a way in. I don't know how she appeared that day you banished her, but she materialized again in my study with everyone in the house."

"And that's why you were so upset?"

"I meant what I said about communing with spirits, but time walking has its uses."

"You could've asked, Elijah."

"Laura would've known. It had to be this way."

"What if I couldn't do it?"

"You said your mother came to you just before I arrived. She came again for your transition. I saw the line in the book. She found me. She knew I was your harnesser. You said she came every time you were in trouble, so I had a hunch she'd come again. She's your familiar on the other side."

"That was some hunch."

Elijah rose to his feet and pulled her with him. "I believed in you."

"Where are we?" One of his men asked behind them.

Celine arched an eyebrow. "I have a hunch."

*****

Elijah turned in a circle, increasingly uncomfortable with the surroundings. "Care to enlighten me, Celine?"

"Mabel."

"Who the fuck is Mabel?"

"My client."

"Can we unharness her?" one of Elijah's men asked.

"Do you have names?" Celine questioned.

Elijah grumbled something he refused to repeat. "Yes. Release her. I never fully broke the connection to her."

Celine swung one arm at the group. "Who are they anyway?"

"They endured the curse with me. They are Unseelie harnessers without mates."

"I didn't think you could harness without being true mates?"

Elijah grinned. "That's why I kept one rope secured to you. First, in case they separated us. Second, because these men couldn't harness you completely."

Celine moved closer. "Don't ever do that again."

"Or what?"

"I'll send you freefalling through the Domain of Souls."

"I love it when you threaten me."

Celine chuckled when he yanked her against his chest.

"Now why are we here, and who is Mabel?"

"Mabel was my client. The one who sent me to find out why her husband died. I think she set me up, and I think Laura is behind it all."

"Why?"

"Because if you hadn't shown up, I wouldn't be here."

Elijah considered the hypothesis from every angle. It made sense except for one problem. "How did Laura know about you?"

"My mother was a necromancer. She tormented my mother along with her legion, losing the chance when my mom passed."

"How would Laura know your mother was a necromancer? Or anything about the Unseelie?"

Celine's mouth pursed even though he already knew the answer. "Don't make me say it, Elijah."

"She used me. Bitch," he hissed.

"I'm sorry. I know you cared for her."

He lifted one hand. "That means she approached me, knowing I had a mate. She premeditated the entire thing to keep us apart. Fucking bitch from hell." Elijah turned in another circle. "Back to the beginning. You said back to the beginning. We're in Salem."

Celine faced his men. "Can you harness a demon?"

They glanced at each other, but one of them nodded. "My name is Vincent, and yes, we can, although it's not full proof. Demons aren't technically souls."

"I know you're all searching for your mates, but you came when Elijah called. I don't ask this for me, but for the Fae realm. Will you help me?"

"What the fuck, Celine? These are my men. You rely on me."

Her head tilted as sadness swept through her beautiful eyes. "I need you to harness me when I leave my body."

136

"No. You can't alter the timeline, Celine. You know this. Anything you change could cause irreparable damage."

She laid one palm over his heart. "I'm not going to change anything that's happened because then I wouldn't have met you."

*****

How did she do that? One minute he wanted to shake her, and the next she gripped his heart in her dainty palm. "You can't go there again. They'll be waiting for you. I'm surprised they aren't here already."

"They don't know yet. We left them in Fae. Laura only knew I was a necromancer. She suspected and hoped I could time walk but wasn't sure. I need a portal to Seattle."

"Why?"

"Ara's mate."

"You better start explaining, Celine."

"Bianca."

"Fucking hell. What did she put you up to?"

"Ara's mate was attacked the moment I was."

Elijah inhaled a deep breath. "I'm going to pretend I don't know we have to approach the fucking Dragon Syndicate to save a male dragon on the edge of insanity they think has mind sickness when it's really demons."

"Well, you go on and pretend, but I'm going to save Ara's mate, so we can close the portal in the Fae realm."

"You don't even know where you're going!"

"Seattle. I know that much. The Dragon Syndicate shouldn't be that hard to find."

"What? You think they put a neon sign out?"

"No, but I'm sure you know."

"No unnecessary risks, Celine. If I sense anything, I'll yank you out so fast you'll get whiplash."

A bright smile spread across her sexy face.

"Stop grinning at me, Celine. I'm not happy about this, and still slightly confused."

Her slim arms wrapped his waist, and he rolled his eyes. And when she nuzzled his chest, his dick instantly hardened. "Stop that shit," he grumbled even as one hand slid over her head.

"Why didn't you just take us to Seattle?"

Her sigh told him there was more.

"I think Mabel was Laura's mother, and her father was the spirit I followed."

"Go on."

"You said Laura was addicted, and that she went too far one night."

"And?"

"What would any parent do to get their child back? If she appeared to us, she could've appeared to them. In their grief, they would've done anything. I think Laura used it against them. Her father crossed over, but the mother, Mabel, stayed on this side."

"So, she could approach you." Elijah sighed at the sick plan.

"How did you know, Elijah? How did you know I needed you?"

"Bianca brought me the tourmaline, your talisman."

"Bianca is a Druid Goddess. She works with the Druid Council, right? You said they can sense the slightest hint of magic?"

"Yes."

Celine tapped her chin. "Bianca said she could only guide. She knew my mother, but couldn't interfere with life and death. My mother traveled to the future. She knew you were my harnesser. I saw it in her book before you destroyed it."

Elijah chuckled. "And she told Danu or Bianca. The Druid Council and Bianca guided the hell out of us."

"They had to intervene, or we wouldn't have met. Laura couldn't have predicted your return, the return of the Unseelie King, but Bianca knew. You were the variable in the plan, but if Laura claimed my body first and approached you before we met..."

"I wouldn't have been the wiser, and she would've ruled both worlds."

"That means Ara's mate was a variable as well."

"And we're here to what? Find out about Laura's family? Does it matter now?" Elijah frowned.

"If they knew about me, then they knew about Ara's mate. The entire dragon nation could be at risk, since he and Ara haven't claimed each other."

"Tobias and Ara claimed each other before the war."

Celine's eyes widened. "You knew Ara's mate?"

"I knew him. He was a great king, and Ara was destined to be his queen."

"And she's existed all this time without him?"

"There's a reason. Right now, we need to worry about your client. I met Laura years ago. How would the mother still live?"

"Mabel came to me several months ago, and I know her address," Celine proudly stated.

"You can't approach her, Celine. It doesn't make sense, anyway. Mabel couldn't have lived that long."

"Not without help. Or if she's something more? I need to know how she's still alive and how they're communicating. A quick peek in the window."

"No. She knows you."

"He's right, Celine," Vincent stated, coming alongside them. "But she doesn't know me."

Celine smiled brightly at Elijah's handsome friend. "I like you."

"Don't fucking look at him like that," Elijah grumbled.

*****

Five minutes later, they stepped through a portal Elijah opened, several houses down from Mabel's house in the suburbs. Vincent continued along the sidewalk with two of Elijah's friends.

Celine froze in place and clasped Elijah's hand, preventing him from going any farther. She shook her head. "Something's not right."

140

The house was quiet and dark, as if empty, but something or someone was there. Her head tilted, studying the small cottage with colorful flower shrubs lining the front. Her heart thudded loudly in her chest. Panic clogged her throat and slid through her veins like ice. "Call them back. Call them back now, Elijah."

A shrill scream split the quiet night. Everyone covered their ears and lifted their faces to the thing rising from the roof of the house. Silver hair floated beside her slight frame, and a black, tattered dress descended to her bare feet.

"Oh, my God. She's a banshee. Mabel is a banshee. No wonder she knew and is still here." Celine ran toward Vincent and the other two men just as the banshee screamed again. The windows on her small cottage exploded outward, car alarms went off, leaves fell from the trees, and the entire area trembled.

Elijah grabbed her from behind and positioned them against an enormous oak tree just as Mabel rotated, searching the area with glowing white eyes.

"Don't make a sound," Elijah barely whispered against her ear. "She sensed our arrival."

Another scream pierced the night, and lights in random houses turned on. Celine peeked around the side of the tree to see Mabel fly in the opposite direction, wailing and screeching.

Elijah stopped her when she took a step. "Give it a minute to be sure she doesn't return."

"Where's Vincent and the other men?"

"Hiding just like we are."

Five more minutes passed, the neighborhood seemed to quiet again, lights turned off, people went back to bed, and that's when they returned to the sidewalk.

"How didn't I know?" Celine asked herself more than anyone.

"Banshees can sense the death of loved ones. They are Unseelie. That's how Laura knew everything, which also means she was half banshee. It all makes sense now. I wondered how she could enter the Fae realm."

"Are there more?"

"Maybe. I don't know. It was rumored Tristan's father saw one before his wife died, and again before his death."

"How terrible to know of your husband's and daughter's deaths, but not be able to do anything about it, and live with the knowledge."

"The only power they possess is the premonition of death. Banshees are tortured souls. They can scare the living daylights out of you and foresee death, but that's about it."

Celine and Elijah crossed to the other side of the street as Vincent and his men continued toward the house. They peered through the windows but returned in a hurry.

"Spirit board," Vincent spoke, approaching them. "She's using the board to communicate with the dead. Should we take it?"

"Absolutely not," Celine hissed. "Don't touch it. The user connects to the board. Open a portal to Seattle. Hurry, Elijah. Ara's mate is Laura's last chance."

Everyone glanced over their shoulders when they heard Mabel's scream again and rushed into the safe light of the portal.

*****

Celine pointed to the podium of people in blue and red robes glaring at her. She turned to him with a frown. "Please tell me we aren't standing before the Dragon Syndicate?"

Elijah shrugged and grinned. "Oops."

Vincent snorted somewhere behind him.

Gasps of shock sounded from the podium until one man rose to his feet. "What is the meaning of this, Elijah Drake, King of the Unseelie?"

"Oh, you know me?" Elijah bowed at the waist, then gestured to his right. "May I introduce my mate, Celine?"

"Yes, I heard you claimed your queen. Poor girl. And that the Druids removed your wretched curse."

Celine snarled at him, but he was all smiles. "You heard correctly."

"Why have you approached us?" the man demanded.

"We seek audience with the one you call Tobias," Elijah said. "The King of the Dragons."

The council broke into whispers, glancing between each other until the man who stood shook his head. "That's not possible. He's ill."

143

"I didn't know dragons were susceptible to illness?" Elijah taunted. "What is your name, councilman?"

"I am Levi. Remember, you're addressing the entire council, King of the Unseelie. Dragons don't have a king anymore."

Elijah held up one finger. "Not true. King Aramand is on Dragon Mountain as we speak."

Levi's eyes narrowed to thin slits. "And?"

Celine cleared her throat at his side and stepped forward. "Please sir. We have reason to suspect Tobias isn't ill, but under demonic attack."

"Impossible," the man practically yelled. "Leave now before I have you thrown out. You necromancers are nothing but dirt and not welcome here."

Celine jerked, but Elijah tensed. No one spoke to his mate like that, except him. "Listen here, motherfucker. What Celine says is the truth, and if you pulled your snouts out of your asses long enough, you'd know dragons don't lose their minds from illness. They are immortal badasses with nasty tempers, true, but sickness...not possible. I always wondered how you were so quick to condemn your own species. I suggest you listen to my mate. They voted you fuckers on that podium to help, not lock dragons in dungeons like criminals. The isolation tips them over the edge."

"How dare you!" the man barked. "You know nothing about dragons."

"I know enough," Elijah yelled back.

The double doors to the room burst open at the same moment. Jax marched in with Ara at his side. "They refuse to let us see Tobias. You're wasting your time."

Celine ran to Ara but turned on the council members. "Shame on you all. I'm telling you the truth because they attacked me at the same time. What kind of monsters are you? Tobias is your king!"

"Lies," the man yelled, jumping from the podium. "How dare you come in here, necromancer! You should've died like your interfering mother!"

The entire building went dead silent.

"What did you say?" Elijah growled, pacing in front of the man.

Everyone turned when another voice whispered in the chamber.

Elijah flexed as his soul expanded. White ropes flung from his body, grasped the man by the waist and neck, and lifted him off the floor. "You dare threaten my mate, demon. How do you know anything about Celine's mother?"

"Unseelie trash. You were once the undead, so you know how much better it was to be a vampire. Why do you care?"

The remaining members of the syndicate rose to their feet, but a female dragon was the one to speak. "You always wanted more power, Levi. Was it worth your soul?"

"Better than hiding what we are, chasing rogue dragons, and trying to maintain order in this filthy human realm. I should be the king. It was promised to me if..."

"If you locked Tobias away," the councilwoman provided.

"I'm going to fucking fry your ass," Ara grumbled, shifting instantly. Her red dragon rose in the chamber, stomping the floor, shaking the entire structure.

Elijah held Levi until he saw the fire expand from Ara's dragon's nostrils, and her mouth opened full of flames. "Duck," he yelled, releasing Levi to grab Celine.

Fire engulfed Levi's body. A black, smoky figure rose from his charred remains. It screeched and circled the room before disappearing through the ceiling.

"For fuck's sake," Elijah yelled. "They infiltrated your Syndicate."

Celine stared at Ara's massive red dragon. "We've got to get to Tobias, or she'll destroy the world."

Elijah chuckled. "Ara has more control than you think."

The female Syndicate member landed on the floor next to Drake's ashes as Ara shifted to her human body. After providing Ara with a robe, she turned to Elijah and the rest of the group. "My name is Deana. Follow me."

"It's not what I thought," Celine commented on the elevator.

"Dungeons and moats?" Elijah teased.

She moved closer to his side, seeking his strength even if he didn't know it. The idea of traveling into the Domain of Souls had her spooked and uncertain. His fingers brushed and linked with hers as if he knew her inner turmoil and offered private comfort in the crowded elevator.

Her gaze dropped to their joined hands. Elijah never told her, in words, how he felt. That day in his study, he'd begged for her confession, and it was right when she succumbed and offered it freely. She understood his desperation now.

The tunic barely contained his tight chest, and the black tourmaline suspended from his neck, reminding her of their bond. He said he fought it, but she was glad he lost the battle. *So beautiful.* He had become her everything, but was she his?

Slowly his face turned, and black eyes lowered to stare at her. White hair surrounded the epitome of masculinity. His tongue slid across his bottom lip, and her body responded. His gaze dropped to her breasts, then lifted to her necklace. With his free hand, he touched it, fingers grazing her bare flesh exposed by the V-neck of the tunic.

Unspoken emotion flooded her, comforting and compassionate. *"It'll be okay. I'm always with you,"* she heard his deep voice speak in her mind.

The elevator doors opened, and she inhaled a deep breath of courage. Thankful he didn't release her hand, she followed him into a white marble corridor. Many cells lined the passage, but they were enormous, reaching hundreds of feet into the air. Roars of rage echoed throughout the cavities, and tremors vibrated the floor beneath her feet.

"How many?" she asked Deana.

"Too many. There are multiple levels. Some submit themselves freely, and some are hunted."

"Why?"

"After centuries of existing without their mates, they can't endure being alone anymore. We're meant to live in pairs. Fire and water, tempering each other."

Celine shook her head. "So, the sickness is real?"

Deana's back stiffened even as her shoulders slumped. "I questioned it, but listened to Levi when I should've questioned it more. He and his followers were persuasive in their argument. I don't have that answer."

Elijah touched Celine's lower back. "Loneliness doesn't always mean insane."

"Fire and water?" Celine asked.

Ara glanced over her shoulder. "I'm fire. Tobias is water. I've struggled to hold my rage for centuries, but it's possible."

Deana halted in the corridor and pivoted to face everyone. "It'll be a shock when you see Tobias. He hasn't been here long, but it ravaged his body. I've never seen a dragon male in such a state. He speaks jumbled words, and he covers the walls in symbols none of us recognize. He has moments of awareness, but most of the time he's mad. We've done everything we can to soothe him without success."

Celine recognized the pain on Deana's face because she had experienced it with her mother. "Levi called my mother interfering?"

Deana frowned. "Because your mother delivered the warning before her death. Levi and his followers dismissed it. I apologize, Celine."

Elijah's hand squeezed hers.

Deana pivoted and continued deeper inside the fortress.

No one spoke when Deana stopped before a cell lined with iron bars. "Tobias," she softly crooned. "You have visitors."

Celine almost stepped on Elijah's feet when the whispers began, and a man came into view. Tangled, dark hair slid to his waist in knots, dirt covered his exposed skin, and his clothing hung in tatters from his body. Bright blue eyes darted between everyone, pausing on her. "Necromancer," he hissed in a gravelly voice. "How good to see you again."

 Fear paralyzed Celine. This was the demon that attacked her in the Domain of Souls.

Ara rushed toward the bars, but Jax caught her at the same moment Tobias lunged for her.

Elijah's hard body moved in front of her, blocking her view of Tobias. "Don't show fear, Celine. Tobias is not under torment; he lives within torment. He's fully possessed. I've seen it before."

"The stone hangs from his neck, Elijah. I saw it," Celine whispered.

"We'll get it."

"How do I get the demon out of him? I don't know what to do."

"We give it a reason to leave."

Celine's eyes lifted. "It wanted me, Elijah."

"That's not Mabel's husband. That's Laura."

Celine worked the details out. It was Laura all along. Mabel was Banshee, so she must have been searching for her husband, but he'd already passed into the Domain of Peace. Laura took the husband's place. "And she wants my body, my life. She knew we'd come here. Loosen the harness, Elijah."

"No."

"It's the only way."

He swore as all the harnessers surrounded him and her. Vincent laid one hand on her shoulder from behind. "Celine is right, Elijah. Loosen your hold and walk away. The demon will believe you've abandoned her."

He shook his head even as she pressed one hand against his chest. "Tighten the harness at the last possible second, Elijah. I'll return Laura to the Domain of Souls. Give my diamond to Ara to close the doorway in the Fae realm."

"I can't do it, Celine. I can't walk away from you. Everything in me says this isn't the way."

"And you won't," Tristan said, stepping through a portal outside the circle with Dagen and Stevie.

"How'd you know?" Celine asked.

Tristan motion to Stevie. "The oracle told me."

When Stevie approached the group with her palm open, Elijah withdrew the stones and placed them in her hand. Before she left, she glanced at Celine. "You're stronger than you realize. Trust your instincts and give that bitch hell."

"Another queen," Tobias hissed. "Aren't you going to speak to me, Stevie? You were my favorite. Oh, the things I could've done in that demigoddess body. Where's Nena? She should've come too."

Stevie paused.

Elijah shook his head. "Go, Stevie. We will manage this. You know what to do."

After Tristan, Dagen, and Stevie left through the portal, Celine turned to the group. "Everyone leaves, except Elijah, Jax, and Ara."

*****

"I need a chair placed before the bars of Tobias' cell," Celine whispered in Elijah's ear. "Loosen the harness, but not fully."

There was no way he was going to loosen anything with that bitch just waiting for an opportunity. "No. Final answer. Don't fuck with me on this, Celine."

"So cranky." Celine kissed his cheek and lowered from her tiptoes, but he caught her.

"No unnecessary risks, Celine."

"Of course, my king. Did you alert Wilma and the other harnesser couples?"

"I did."

"Perfect. Let's do it."

He wanted to bust her ass or fuck her senseless, but laid her over his arm in front of Demon Laura, kissing her until she moaned, and her fingers threaded into his hair.

"What was that for?" Celine asked.

"Just letting the bitch watching us know who I belong to."

"I knew who you belonged to in the club," Celine teased.

"You think," he smirked, setting her on her feet.

After a chair was positioned close to the cell, Celine sat down with Elijah behind her.

Demon Laura laughed. "You think to outsmart me, necromancer?"

"Don't speak to it," Elijah warned.

Demon Laura sat cross-legged on the floor. "So, are we playing a game, King of the Unseelie? Maybe chess with your mate's soul?"

Celine relaxed the moment his hands slid over her shoulders. He knew what she was doing, but Demon Laura didn't know.

Elijah squeezed her shoulder. "Preparing for a trip, Laura."

"So, you know it's me? I'm flattered. I never could trick you, lover."

"I'm not your lover," Elijah growled. "You tricked me, used me, whatever you want to call it."

"And you were eager to have me. We could be together again." Demon Laura licked her lips.

"You were the greatest mistake of my life, Laura. We won't happen again. We never should've happened."

"Oh, I don't know. We were sizzling hot together." Demon Laura smacked her lips.

"Just a flash burn, Laura. Quick to heal and easily forgotten."

Demon Laura's eyes narrowed. "Careful, Unseelie."

"Or what?" Elijah asked, the ropes of his soul expanding in white light.

"So pretty, Elijah. I remember those ropes. Your harness won't keep her from me. I'll have her body, and I'll rule as queen of everything, even if I have to kill you."

Elijah kissed the top of Celine's head, but his gaze remained on Demon Laura. "You're nothing but a lower-level demon with a fucking jealous streak."

Demon Laura jumped to her feet. "As soon as I kill you, she's mine."

Celine's soul rose to hover beside her physical body. She purposely floated through the cell bars before Demon Laura. "How awful to spend eternity wanting to live again. To never know true love. I feel sorry for you, but I pity your mother even more."

"You're out of your body, queen, so it's mine," Demon Laura hissed.

"Silly demon. You can't possess a body that's been fully harnessed. I assumed you knew since you tormented my mother."

Demon Laura turned in a circle, laughing maniacally. "I possessed this one."

"No, you're sharing it, but that's it. Tobias is still there. If he dies, where will you go? Bouncing from body to body? Continue to haunt and be a nuisance? You should get yourself some chains," Celine taunted.

Demon Laura grasped at her spirit and screeched when Celine moved away.

All the gloating was too much for any demon. Celine shimmered until she disappeared, her voice echoing off the chamber walls. "See you in the Domain of Souls, Laura. Come get your crown."

Would Laura take the bait? Elijah waited patiently, and he didn't wait long. Tobias collapsed on the floor when Laura flew from his body in pursuit of Celine.

Deana opened the cell, Ara and Jax rushed inside. Wilma and the harnessed pairs quickly rushed into the cell and surrounded them, clapped once, and raised a secure dome over Tobias, Ara, and Jax. The dome continued to rise until it encapsulated the entire building. There was no possible way Laura could return.

He watched Ara carefully remove the necklace from Tobias' neck and toss it to Jax.

Jax opened a portal and ran through it.

Elijah lifted his face to the ceiling, closed his eyes, and allowed the true power of the Unseelie harnesser and descendant of Nephilim to expand into the Domain of Souls in full physical body.

Chapter 8

Tristan, Nena, Dagen, and Stevie snuck to the cave in The Opposite where the demons congregated. The chanting had increased in strength since the last time they were here, but Stevie and Nena knew what to look for.

Dirt and brush concealed everything, making it difficult to locate the keys, but the four of them covered the ground quickly.

"Here," Stevie pointed.

Dagen kneeled beside her and wiped the dirt away. "Are you sure? I don't see it."

Tristan lowered in a crouch at the base of the cliff with Nena standing at his side. The pregnancy made it difficult for her.

Stevie touched a crevice. "I saw it in a vision. Hand me the stones."

Tristan quickly dropped all three in her hand. "It looks like the Unseelie diamond."

Stevie fumbled with it until it slid perfectly into the slot, and the symbols closest lit white. "That's it. Find the rest."

Dagen pointed over her head to the slope on the cave's face. "There. Give me the other two stones. I'll have to shift to reach it." Once he took his Lycan form, he fumbled with the stones until the Fae peridot popped into the slot. Bright green light expanded halfway over the face of the cavern.

Tristan glanced at the other side. "That means the other two slots are over there."

Nena opened a portal. "This way, so they don't see us."

Tristan found the slot for the Lycan moonstone. With a twist, it popped in place and blue lighted the symbols.

Nena glanced at Tristan with a worried expression. "The dragon stone. We can't close it without it, and we're almost out of time."

As soon as the words left her mouth, she doubled over. The demonic chanting turned to shrieks. "The baby, Tristan. I'm cramping."

He gathered her in his arms when she covered her ears.

Wind tore through the land, ripping shrubs from the ground and flowers from their stalks. Demons flung themselves against the partial barrier.

"We've got to leave," Tristan yelled. "Nena needs the dragon pools. The barrier won't hold without the last stone."

Dagen gathered Stevie to his chest when a massive black dragon appeared from a portal, claws piercing the earth. Enormous wings spread on either side of its body as it approached the cave, spewing fire from its nostrils.

The demons wailed and moaned, backing away.

With one massive talon, it slammed the dragon stone into the last crevice. Orange light filled the remaining space. All markings flashed three times, and a barrier resembling white fire spread across the face of the cave.

Demons screamed in rage, but they couldn't pass through it.

The wind settled. Jax transitioned to man.

Everyone rushed to him. Dagen offered his shirt to his naked father-in-law.

Tristan scooped Nena into his arms. "I'm taking Nena to the dragon pools."

Jax opened another portal, and together, the five of them went through.

Tristan immediately jumped into the nearest pool. Nena sighed and smiled. "I'm okay. Celine? Ara?"

Jax frowned. "Ara is with Tobias. Celine and Elijah are just starting."

Chapter 9

The first level of the Domain of Souls was peaceful. Spirits shuffled in the white abyss. Celine tilted her head, watching them, accepting them, realizing that death was part of life, and she didn't belong here.

She floated for what seemed like minutes until she heard the scream of her nemesis breaching the Domain of Souls. Although the middle or second domain wasn't any place she wanted to go, she ascended to the next level slowly.

Chaos dominated the middle domain, and she held perfectly still, observing as souls whipped throughout the space in frantic fashion. It was obvious the group sealed the doorway into the Fae realm, since there were so many here. They refused to rise into the upper domain of peace, the knowledge of their human existence erased, and the chance to live again gone forever. She understood, but they did this to themselves.

Her lips firmed when they began circling her, chanting, some whispering obscenities in their haunting voices. These were Laura's followers, those who sought death for answers, and regretted their decision, those who wanted a second chance, and the damned who fought to avoid judgment.

Laura's face passed before her, and she frowned at her grotesque appearance. In this place, concealment wasn't possible. Black eyes, jagged teeth, blackened souls were the mark of the demon, and they had no business here among those seeking peace.

Celine refused to cower or try to hide. There was no place to hide, anyway.

"You're a fool, necromancer."

Laura's voice slithered through her corporeal form, taunting and with cruelty. Hate and jealousy ruled her spirit, flowing from her in waves.

"The Unseelie King would rather be the undead, the vampire without a mate. He doesn't love. Why do you think he never said it? I know because he never said it to me either."

The words hurt because there may be a hint of truth to them, magnifying the doubt already in her mind. Celine still didn't respond.

"Selfish and self-serving. He'll leave you broken, as he did me. He'll never love you, necromancer."

Celine waited, listened, refusing to converse with a liar.

"Such a hopeless romantic. I was your age when I met him. He swore to protect me but left me here. The Unseelie are cursed beings. You're cursed. Your mother was cursed. And your father was weak."

"Because they loved?" Celine questioned. "Because they cared?"

Laura halted directly in front of her and snapped her rotten teeth together. "Love is a lie."

Celine floated a little closer to her. "No. You're a lie. Everything you've done has been a lie. You're an abomination, Laura, and you don't belong here."

Laura and the other demons screamed so loud she thought her corporeal ears might burst.

"You know nothing, necromancer, and are just as addicted to being here as I'm. How many times did you seek answers from the dead?"

"Tell me what knowledge you have that I can't live without, Laura."

"I know Elijah belongs to me! I'm his queen! Think about it, necromancer. He brought you here. He gave you everything except love. He'll abandon you. He's deceived you."

Celine forced herself to remain calm even as her heart lurched. It wasn't true. He wouldn't use her like that. Their bond was the proof. "Lies, demon. You offer nothing but lies."

Laura hovered before her. "Am I lying? You're not sure, are you?"

Doubt was the demon's greatest weapon alongside fear, and Celine couldn't say she wasn't replaying every event. Her spiritual body twisted when the demons began passing through her one after another, screaming and chanting in their tongue, promising death and revenge.

Overwhelmed by the attack, Celine closed her eyes and allowed the middle domain to cradle her body. Elijah would come. He wouldn't betray her.

*****

They were wearing her down, making her doubt. Elijah listened to the entire conversation from his position in the lower domain, directly below them. And when they attacked her, rage tempered with compassion filled his body. He wouldn't allow this to go on. They sealed the doorway into Fae. It was time.

He rose through the barrier to the middle domain, wrapped one arm around Celine's corporeal form, and gently coaxed her spirit into his chest, cradling her against his soul where she would be protected.

Laura wailed and circled him, her wispy body trailing like a comet. "How are you here? And in physical form?"

"I'm Unseelie, a descendent of the Nephilim."

The moment the last word left his mouth, black wings exploded from his shoulder blades and spread on either side of his body.

162

"No," the demons wailed in unison.

His face lifted when light penetrated the ceiling of the middle barrier. White wings dipped below the surface, and shards of gold drifted in the expanse, binding to the demons.

"To the doorway," Laura screeched, but Elijah lashed one rope from his soul to hers.

"No, Laura. The doorway was closed. There's no escape for you."

"The dragons!" she screamed in panic. "My legion will go into the dragons."

But Elijah held firm. "Tobias is safe. The dragons are safe. You'll never penetrate the harnesser's protective dome."

"How could you?" she moaned when an angel lowered behind her. "I love you."

Elijah shook his head, and his tie to her soul retracted. "Lies aren't love, but manipulation. I harnessed the one who loves me. You chose your fate."

Laura's mouth opened with a ghastly moan, but the angels jerked her and the remaining demons through the upper barrier.

One angel remained, and Elijah bowed with respect to his ancestor. When he lifted his head, the angel rose into the upper and final domain. The whitish expanse of the middle domain once again was quiet, with souls meandering toward the peace they earned.

Slowly, he descended into the lower level and returned to the human world, where Celine's body waited to be reunited with its soul.

Wilma stood silently by as he gently withdrew Celine's spirit from within and placed it over her body.

Her eyes fluttered open. "For a moment, I thought you lied again," she barely whispered.

Elijah leaned over her, just above her lips. "I don't lie, necromancer."

A bright smile spread across her face as he scooped her into his arms.

"Is she okay?" Ara asked from beneath the dissipating dome. "Is it over?"

The harnessed pairs left the cell. Elijah faced his old friend, with Celine cradled in his arms. "It's over."

Ara instantly shifted, scooped Tobias from the ground, and burst through the ceiling. Debris crashed into the cell.

"Damn dragons," he grumbled.

"Take her home, Elijah."

His eyebrow arched at his old friend. The thought of offering his thanks to Wilma crossed his mind until a smirk on her wrinkled face brought a scowl instead. "I hate you, old crone."

She cackled behind him as he stepped through a portal.

Chapter 10

Elijah paused before his home with Celine in his arms. Sound asleep, she snuggled into his chest with one hand over his heart.

Sunlight broke the horizon, chasing the shadows away. Home never looked so right. The dark fairies danced from one rose bush to another, and the blooms thrived under their care. Black butterflies and odd birds colored the landscape with their haunting beauty. The trickle of water cascading over rocks provided welcoming peace.

The home of the Unseelie King and Queen was stunning in its dark beauty, and the woman in his arms was responsible. He never thought to have this again after existing as a vampire. Love, home, and family were things he'd ceased hoping for.

His gaze dropped to Celine, noticing the dark circles under her eyes. She was young, but wise. She believed in him when no one else did, and she loved him when no one else could.

A shriek pierced the peaceful moment, and he searched the forest surrounding his home. A growl rumbled from his chest when a figure streaked through the trees and over his house to float before him.

Banshee Mabel hovered not six feet from his position. Tear stains streaked her pale face, and white eyes bore into him.

"For fuck's sake," he grumbled, hefting Celine tighter against his chest. "I'm sick of fighting. Can't I have one damn day, Banshee?"

"Thank you."

It came out as more of a moan, and his head tilted. He never met Laura's parents and was a bit confused. "For what?"

"Thank you for ending my torment, Unseelie King and Queen."

Elijah could only watch as she lowered until her feet touched the ground. She dropped to her knees in a show of respect.

"Get up," he ordered.

Her face lifted.

"She used you, too." It wasn't a question, but a statement.

The Banshee nodded, black tears streaming over her face. "It's my fault. I was Banshee, a cursed being who wanted a normal life. I took a human as a mate, and we had a child. I loved my daughter, but suffering and

166

questions about death consumed her. Please forgive me."

"You aren't responsible for another's actions. We all have free will."

Elijah glanced at Celine when she stirred. A bright smile spread, illuminating her face and his world. "Put me down."

He sat her on her feet but refused to let her leave his side.

"Celine, please forgive me," the Banshee wailed.

"Forgiven," Celine answered, trying to leave the shelter of his arms, which he refused. "Come home, Banshee. You're Unseelie. Your husband and daughter passed into the Domain of Peace."

The Banshee lifted in the air so fast, so high, wailing, shrieking, and crying, that Elijah and Celine both had to look up.

"Good God. She'd wake the fucking dead," he grumbled.

Celine chuckled at his side. "Such a grumpy king."

He lifted his mate against his chest, front to front. "You should be afraid of me."

Celine cupped both cheeks with her warm palms. "I think you're all bark and no bite, Unseelie King."

He playfully nipped at her lips, sliding his tongue across the plump flesh. "Careful or you'll ruin my nasty reputation."

"The dark king has a reputation to protect?"

Elijah kicked the front door open, stepped inside, and kicked it shut. "I'm about to show you just how dark I can be."

Celine laughed when he started down the staircase. "You don't wear a halo, do you?"

"That smart mouth deserves a smack to the ass."

"It's hot when your wings spread," she winked. "And those ropes between my legs."

Elijah tossed her in the middle of his bed and crawled on top of her, pinning her hands above her head. "You like my wings? I like your tits," he growled, sliding his tongue into her cleavage.

"You bit me the first time and took my blood. Think you could do that on my inner thigh this time?"

He chuckled against her shirt, over her nipple. "Such tasty blood, too. You know, I considered draining you dry at the club."

"Confessions from the king. I think I like it. Why didn't you?"

He swirled his tongue on her nipple, wetting the material, and bit it hard.

"I need to hear the words, King of the Unseelie."

"What words? Haven't we talked enough?"

Celine shrugged even as his tongue continued worshipping her nipple. "You know what I want. There'll be no sex until I get it, either."

"No sex? Really? I don't think you can resist."

168

He could've made the tunic shirt and pants disappear, but prolonged the torture, or pleasure, by peeling each item slowly from her body.

"Be still," he commanded when she squirmed from his hair and fingers tickling her ribcage.

"You need a man bun," she laughed.

"What the fuck is a man bun?" he whispered against one puckered nipple.

Celine tossed her arms over her head when he sucked the rosy nipple between his lips and grazed it with his teeth. She gasped and her knees lifted on either side of his head. "You know. When men wear their hair in a bun on top of their head."

He slid lower, flicked her clit, and blew on it. "You need something to grab onto," he teased, her back arching off the bed. "Something to grab when I lick you like this?" He slowly slid his tongue through her folds. "Is that what you're talking about?"

Her head tossed from side to side.

"Maybe I should install bars with shackles over the bed? You could grip the chains while I fuck your pretty little pussy?"

A deep moan escaped as he slid two fingers into her sheath. Wetness slicked her passage, and her legs spread wider.

"I think you like the idea of bondage, sweet queen. Maybe you have a bit of darkness in you."

"Yes. Like that. Don't stop," she begged when he sucked her clit into his mouth.

Elijah worked her body until she was close to coming and rose above her. "Do you want my dick, Celine?"

Her hands slid across his shoulders and over his biceps. "Yes," she said in a breathy moan. "I want all of you. I need everything, Elijah. I need to know."

His wings expanded the second the engorged head slid between her folds.

Flushed and sensual, she gazed at him with watery, black eyes lit with orange flames.

He lowered until their lips barely touched, pulling her legs around his hips at the same time. Her warm palms cupped his cheeks, and her tongue traced the seam of his lips.

"I love you, Celine."

Tears leaked from the corners of her eyes with the confession, and he thrust inside of her. Her pussy spasmed on his dick, milking him, massaging him as she cried out and orgasmed at the same time. Her magic swirled with featherlight caresses that had him on the edge of control.

"I love you too," she whispered into his mouth.

His dick swelled, and within five thrusts, he filled her, and they both groaned with the release.

His face dropped to the crook of her neck, kissing the smooth flesh while inhaling her sweet scent. Her fingers trailed over his back, and her soft thigh slid against his hips.

"All day, Celine."

"What?"

"We aren't leaving the bed today."

He rolled onto his back, and she cuddled into his side.

"Where'd your wings go?"

He chuckled with his eyes closed. "They have a mind of their own, just like my dick."

Celine's warm breath slid over her his nipple when she chuckled, but she flinched when a scream sounded from somewhere over the house.

"Fucking hell. Are we going to listen to that Banshee for the rest of our lives? Send her crying ass back to the human realm, Celine."

Her small hand smacked his stomach. "Can't perform with the theatrics?"

His eyes snapped open, and he lifted her to straddle his waist.

"You're hard again? Already?" she asked, incredulously.

"All day, baby. I bet I can make you scream louder."

Celine arched one eyebrow, sliding between his legs. "Me first," she teased, her mouth dangerously close to his dick.

Elijah chuckled as she stroked him, but inhaled a deep breath when she flicked the head of his dick, sucked him to the back of her throat, then popped off quickly.

"Let's see if I can make the Unseelie King scream."

EPILOGUE

Celine paused in the sunlight, touching a rosebud with her fingers. The dark fairies fluttered beside her before going back to their task of gardening. She smiled but didn't lift her head when she heard the Banshee's cry from the forest. Mabel had stayed, and Celine hoped she would find a semblance of peace.

Elijah kept her in bed for three days after they returned, and her smile spread so wide it almost hurt at the memories. Tender but aggressive, he made love to her, caressing her body until she writhed beneath him, and growling the most blush-worthy things in her ear.

She glanced over her shoulder at where he stood in the sunshine. Her dark angel was wicked to his core.

Her gaze strayed to the mountains in the distance. Ara still hadn't returned, and no one had heard from her. She only hoped Tobias was on the mend under the care of his mate.

Nena was doing well after remaining in the dragon pools for several days, and Tristan constantly hovered at her side. Dagen and Stevie returned to their Lycan home. Jax regularly flew in the sky, the black dragon finally content with his new shifter form, but restless in a way she thought had something to do with Bianca.

She turned her head slightly when thick arms surrounded her waist.

"What's on your mind?" His deep voice tickled her ear.

"I'm happy. I was thinking of how much I love it here."

"Good. I have a gift for you. Or rather, Hogden and the fairies have a gift for you."

"Hogden? The ogre? Really? A gift for me."

"For their queen."

She chuckled when he tucked one arm over his and led her into the forest. With everything that happened, she hadn't taken the time to explore the woodlands surrounding them. Enormous trees rose and bent at odd angles high into the sky to block the sunshine, and dark green foliage covered the trail. Moss clung to the bark, and flowers in darker tones sprung from the ground everywhere.

"It's enchanting here," she commented, gazing at everything.

Elijah didn't answer but led her toward a clearing where she could see sunlight, Hogden moving about, and more fairies.

House of Unseelie
Kristal Dawn Harris

"Oh my God," she exclaimed when they finally arrived. A gazebo, similar to the one from her home, dominated the center created with crooked wood like the trees in the forest. Sunlight streamed onto the rusted metal roof, and a large bench swing hung inside. Dark purple flower vines climbed the structure, and more of the same circled a tiny pond.

"They wanted to give you a little piece of home since yours exploded."

Hogden grumbled when she ran to him and hugged him. "Thank you, Hogden," she said, stepping away.

"The queen likes?"

Celine glanced over her shoulder at the man she adored. "The queen loves."

The End

Thank you for reading House of Unseelie from the Kings & Queens series. If you love the story, please consider leaving a review and continuing with House of Dragons, the final book in the series. The first chapter is included!

ABOUT THE AUTHOR

Kristal Dawn Harris is a multiple award-winning, RONE nominated, American romance author. She has been married for 30 years and has two children. Kristal finished a degree from Miami University in Accounting Technology, but quickly realized she preferred words over numbers. She is an avid reader and loves darker paranormal romance. Her hobbies include coin collecting, physical fitness, stained-glass art (beginner), poetry, and songwriting.

Kristal writes paranormal, erotic, fantasy, as well as contemporary romance in different lengths. You can find Kristal and signup for her newsletter @Romance Author | Kristal Dawn Harris Author (kristalharris.com)

MORE BOOKS BY THE AUTHOR

The Rings of Faolan-Emeralds
The Rings of Faolan-Rubies
The Burn
The Red Heart
You Stole My Heart
Hand-Carved Wolf
Red Snowflakes
Seduction by Blood
Rise for Me
Blood Bond
Sensuality & Spells
Seducing His Mate
The Dragon's Gift
Black Lotus

Renaissance
Buccaneer
Sinful Negotiations
A Lipstick Christmas
A Lipstick New Year
A Lipstick Valentine
A Lipstick Mardi Gras
Strawberry Country
House of Fae – Kings & Queens
House of Lycan- Kings & Queens
House of Unseelie – Kings & Queens
House of Dragons-Kings & Queens
UPCOMING RELEASE
Whiskey Butterfly
Infinity

Excerpt from Kings and Queens:
House of Dragons

Ara burst through the ceiling of the Dragon Syndicate and streaked through the clouds with Tobias in her clutches, wings spread wide. And it wasn't to save or protect him. He had answers, and she wanted them immediately. Possessed wasn't anything compared to the demon he was about to face.

Where the fuck had he been all this time?

Fire shot from her nostrils when she banked left too close to a cliff. If anyone saw her, they'd assume she'd lost her dragon mind with the reckless way she flew. She hadn't been this pissed since she killed Tristan's bloodthirsty father.

She fumed for two days, dragging her mate's sorry ass from island to island off the coast of Washington. He never once opened his eyes. If his chest didn't move, she'd think he was dead.

A portal formed directly ahead with a thought, and she rushed through it like the hounds of hell gripped her spiked tail. An anguished roar split the Fae night, and her fire burned a hole through an innocent cloud. The twin moons did nothing to calm her spirit. She teetered on the edge of insanity from his betrayal, and his deceit pierced her heart.

The dark, cavernous entrance of her lair appeared on the edge of the cliff, and she plowed inside. No one came to this side of the mountain. This secret space was her private sanctuary.

Tobias scraped the ground below her. She should kill him. The idea caused a war between her rational mind and her heart. A snarl lifted her dragon lips. Damn bond. He would heal, she fumed, and tossed him the rest of the way inside. His ravaged body rolled to land on a sandy spot covered in blankets, half on and half off.

With another roar, she pushed off the side of the rocky wall, rotated, and exited the cave. A lake filled the valley below her lair, and the surrounding forest teemed with animals. She dove headfirst into the water, emerging with a mouthful of fresh fish. After dropping them at the mouth of her lair, she darted into the forest to find her asshole mate fresh meat.

An hour later, she relaxed by a small fire. Meat sizzled above the flames, roasting the way she imagined roasting him. He hadn't moved since she threw him on her sleeping pallet, but he occasionally stirred. Fingers flexed, his eyes twitched beneath his eyelids, and muscles spasmed.

With a huff of annoyance, she stomped to where he lay in his awkward position. Thick legs rested in the sand, but his torso lay on the blanket. She grabbed him by the ankles, grumbling about his size, and positioned his lower body on the pallet.

Narrowed eyes slithered over his muscular form, noticing every detail. Dark hair fell in tangled knots to his waist and winged eyebrows dominated the areas over his eyes. Angular cheekbones and jawline lent him a harsh edge. Cuts and bruises marred his skin. Her chin lifted as she considered carving one more for the collection.

Tobias had definitely matured since she last saw him, even in his present condition.

Dick. Motherfucker. Asshole.

She returned to her fire, his betrayal twisting in her gut. The bitterness from the festering wound seeped into everything. Bianca's warning haunted her.

"And Ara... all is not what it seems. Remember to listen to the heart, not the fire."

How was she supposed to do that? Ara twirled a stick in her hand, breaking it into smaller pieces to toss in the flames. Everyone said he died, killed by Tristan's father. The spear pierced her mind as it pierced his chest. There wasn't a body, but that wasn't unusual considering the nasty magic wielded that fateful day.

Her spiteful gaze drifted to him again. Tobias was her first, her king, and her mate. The moment he thrust inside her and claimed her as his, lightning struck both their backs, and the brand of mates forever burned into their skin. If she could filet hers off, she would.

She'd been faithful when no hope remained. Was he? Dragons mated for life, and she still belonged to him. Fucker. She should be able to touch his mind, but every time she tried, she rammed into a brick wall. A thousand scenarios played out in her head, and none of them helped calm her anger, disgust, and heartbreak.

His sword lay in a crevice behind her, deep in the stone wall, protected by leather. She found it on the battlefield and hid it here where no one could ever find it. The sword belonged to the Dragon King, the true king, and no one else would ever wield the blade again. She made that promise to him out of fealty and devotion.

She pivoted onto her knees and withdrew it from the wall. The stone was missing from the pommel, and the space it occupied a hollow void. One fingertip touched the pointed tip of the blade, sliding over the sharp edge. Ara hissed from the sting when it sliced her skin open.

Tobias moaned, scenting her blood. Her eyes lifted, heat radiating from them. When he thrashed his arms, she couldn't stop herself from going to him. The bloody fingertip slid between his lips. Warmth from his mouth surrounded the digit, and he sucked, pulling more blood from her. Color restored to his cheeks, bruises faded, and many of his wounds closed.

Her eyes shut, remembering every detail of their time together. This man made her a woman. She gave him everything. His strength and confidence once drew people to him, their fierce leader, and she was no exception. They were promised to each other as destined mates, The King and Queen of the Dragons.

A battle horn sounded in her mind from the day Tobias left to fight for their species. The bloody battle lasted three days. Tristan's merciless father tore through Fae, savagely killing anyone he thought stronger. The dragons were a constant thorn in his side, defying him on every issue.

The Dragon Syndicate refused to bow to him, but they met defeat. The Syndicate re-established in the human world, but she avoided them like the fucking cowards they were, leaving her to clean up their mess.

Tristan came to her on the third day of battle, asking for help. At first, she denied him until she felt the spear penetrate her mate's chest through their bond. The pain ripped through her soul, and she fell to her knees when he plummeted from the sky. Everyone she loved died in that battle, even her parents.

In a blind rage, revenge the only thing on her mind, she flew straight and determined along the face of the mountain to where the evil king gloated. Her dragon eyes never wavered when Tristan dropped to his knees.

Trees and vegetation silently bent on her approach. In the king's moment of bloody glory, he didn't realize she was behind him until it was too late.

The fire she unleashed that day was unholy, powerful, and filled with hate. With Tobias dead, there was no one left to curb her anger, her loneliness, or her need for retaliation. The king burned to ash where he stood, and she consumed his bones, ensuring he never rose again.

Tobias tempered her fire, but the well ran dry with the war and his death.

Ara opened her eyes and jerked her finger from his mouth. Her other hand squeezed the pommel of his sword, considering ending his life. She lifted it above him, glaring at the mate who'd betrayed her. The sword sliced through the air, halting above his neck. Her eyes burned with unshed tears as she backed away.

Unable to take his life, she returned the sword to its hiding place and settled by the fire.

Throughout the years, she thought she experienced him, a tingle of awareness, but she learned to ignore it. His ghost lived in her mind, and she survived on the edge, teetering close to insanity without him.

It was a tremendous shock to hear Bianca speak his name in the same sentence as *alive*. And even more of a shock to see him in that cell, tormented by something she couldn't fight.

But thanks to Elijah and Celine, everything was made right except one unanswered question burning in her mind.

Why hadn't Tobias returned to the Fae Kingdom and to her?

She tossed another stick in the flames and kicked one of the round stones surrounding it with her bare foot. She should bathe him and give him more blood to speed his healing. She should do a lot of things, but he didn't deserve it.

Tobias was another reason on a long list why she hated kings.

Will Ara control her fire? Find out in the final book in the Kings & Queens series, House of Dragons!

House of Unseelie
Kristal Dawn Harris

Made in United States
Orlando, FL
28 January 2024

43041013R00104